Francis Turner Palgrave

The Children's Treasury of Lyrical Poetry

Part 1

Francis Turner Palgrave

The Children's Treasury of Lyrical Poetry
Part 1

ISBN/EAN: 9783744766272

Printed in Europe, USA, Canada, Australia, Japan

Cover: Foto ©Andreas Hilbeck / pixelio.de

More available books at **www.hansebooks.com**

Toronto University Library

—

Presented by

Messr. Macmillan & Co.

through the Committee formed in

The Old Country

to aid in replacing the loss caused by

The disastrous Fire of February the 14th 1890

THE

CHILDREN'S TREASURY

OF

LYRICAL POETRY

FIRST PART

SELECTED AND ARRANGED WITH NOTES BY

FRANCIS TURNER PALGRAVE

PROFESSOR OF POETRY IN THE UNIVERSITY OF OXFORD
LATE FELLOW OF EXETER COLLEGE, OXFORD

London
MACMILLAN AND CO.
AND NEW YORK
1889

The Publishers owe their thanks to the liberality of some English copyright owners; and also to Mr. William Cullen Bryant for the use of his two Poems " To a Waterfowl," and " The Death of the Flowers": also to Messrs. James R. Osgood & Co. for permission to print Professor Longfellow's " The Wreck of the Hesperus," from their copyright edition of his works.

First Edition 1875.
Reprinted 1877, 1879, 1880, 1881, 1883, 1884, 1885, 1886, 1888, 1889.

PREFACE

THIS selection is planned for children between nine or ten, and fifteen or sixteen years of age; the pleasure and advantage of the older students in Elementary, and the younger in Grammar and Public Schools, being especially kept in view. As it is meant for their own possession and study, not less than for use as a class-book in the teacher's hand, sufficient notes (it is thought) have been added to render the volume by itself fairly comprehensible to children of average intelligence : and the editor hopes that this object may be his excuse with those who may consider the annotations too numerous.

The scheme of choice followed has produced a selection different from any known to the editor. Suitability to childhood is, of course, the common principle of all. But, this quality secured (so far as individual judgment can), nothing has been here admitted which does not reach a high rank in poetical merit; and the available stores of English poetry have been carefully reviewed for the purpose. The editor's wish has been to collect all songs, narratives, descriptions, or reflective pieces of a lyrical quality, fit to give pleasure, —high, pure, manly, (and therefore lasting)— to children in the stage between early childhood and early youth : and no pieces which are not of this character. Poetry, for poetry's sake, is what

he offers. To illustrate the history of our literature, to furnish specimens of leading or of less-
known poets, to give useful lessons for this or
the other life, to encourage a patriotic temper—
each an aim fit to form the guiding principle of
a selection—have here only an indirect and sub-
sidiary recognition. It is, however, believed that,
so far as the scope of the book coincides with
such other aims, they may be more effectually
served through the powerful operation of really
good poetry, than when made the main object of
a collection.

The standard of ' merit as poetry' (so far as the
editor, aided by some friends distinguished by good
judgment and scholarship, may have been success-
ful in preserving it), has excluded a certain number
of popular favourites. But the standard of ' suitability to childhood,' as here understood, has excluded many more pieces : pictures of life as it seems
to middle-age—poems coloured by sentimentalism
or morbid melancholy, however attractive to readers
no longer children—love as personal passion or
regret (not love as the groundwork of action)—
artificial or highly allusive language—have, as a
rule, been held unfit. The aim has been to shun
scenes and sentiments alien from the temper of
average healthy childhood, and hence of greater
intrinsical difficulty than poems containing un-
usual words. Hence, although the rules of choice
have given this book, as compared with many of
its predecessors, an unfamiliar air, yet it is believed
that the contents will in fact prove ultimately at
least as comprehensible to children between the
ages specified.

Poems suitable for readers in the latter half of these years are marked with a star in the index. Some pieces will be found admitted as examples leading up to the poetry appropriate to later education and the experience of life ; but, looking to the small size of the collection, it has not been thought desirable to attempt ranging the contents in order of composition or of relative difficulty.

A few omissions have been made in order to render a poem more suitable for childhood, or to escape encroachment on the field of distinctly devotional verse ; others, more copiously, when the poem could be thus strengthened in a vivid effectiveness. The North-country Ballads have thus been greatly shortened ; a child (in the editor's judgment), especially one unfamiliar with dialect, being more likely to appreciate afterwards their charming antique garrulity, and the repetitions of phrase proper to orally-published poetry, if presented first with a tale in our more condensed modern manner. When, as here, poetry for poetry's sake is concerned, extracts in general appear wholly unsatisfactory to the editor ; they are like fragments barbarously broken from statues. Such only have, therefore, been included which form in themselves complete works of art.

The rule that no piece should be admitted, unless reaching a high rank in poetical merit, if carried out successfully, will have rendered this book fit also for older readers. Such will know that the treasures here collected are but a few drops from an ocean, unequalled in wealth and variety by any existing literature ; that many illustrious names are, necessarily, altogether absent; that many

others receive but a meagre and imperfect repre-
sentation.   Among the five (surviving) Imperial
poets of the Western world, England claims
two ; but how faintly does a selection, limited
as this, present the splendour of Shakespeare and
Milton ! Descending one or two steps, if Wordsworth and Scott, within this century, are fairly
shown in a single region of their power, Keats,
Shelley, Byron, Crabbe, on different grounds,
must be nearly or wholly undisplayed. But, in
truth, no selection should be planned or accepted
as able to do more than open a glimpse into the
' Elysian fields ' of song.   Pleasant as has been
the task of forming this book, in the hope that it
may, in itself, prove a pleasure and a gain to the
dear English and English-speaking children, all the
world over,—yet the editor will hold his work but
half fulfilled, unless they are tempted by it to go
on and wander, in whatever direction their fancy
may lead them, through the roads and winding
ways of this great and glorious world of English
poetry.   He aims only at showing them the path,
and giving them a little foretaste of our treasures: —

To-morrow to fresh woods, and pastures new.

F. T. P.

MAY: 1875

The Children's Treasury

ᐧ 1 ᐧ

A LAUGHING SONG

WHEN the green woods laugh with the voice of joy,
And the dimpling stream runs laughing by;
When the air does laugh with our merry wit,
And the green hill laughs with the noise of it;

When the meadows laugh with lively green,　　　5
And the grasshopper laughs in the merry scene;
When Mary, and Susan, and Emily,
With their sweet round mouths sing, 'Ha, ha, he!'

When the painted birds laugh in the shade,
Where our table with cherries and nuts is spread : 10
Come live, and be merry, and join with me
To sing the sweet chorus of 'Ha, ha, he!'

W. Blake

ᐧ 2 ᐧ

THE PET LAMB

THE dew was falling fast, the stars began to blink;
I heard a voice; it said, 'Drink, pretty creature,
　　drink!'
And looking o'er the hedge, before me I espied
A snow-white mountain lamb, with a maiden at its
　　side.

B

Nor sheep, nor kine were near ; the lamb was all
    alone,   5
And by a slender cord was tether'd to a stone ;
With one knee on the grass did the little maiden
    kneel,
While to that mountain lamb she gave its evening
    meal.

The lamb, while from her hand he thus his supper
    took,
Seem'd to feast with head and ears ; and his tail
    with pleasure shook :   10
'Drink, pretty creature, drink!' she said in such a tone
That I almost received her heart into my own.

'Twas little Barbara Lewthwaite, a child of beauty
    rare !
I watch'd them with delight, they were a lovely pair;
Now with her empty can the maiden turn'd away ; 15
But ere ten yards were gone, her footsteps did she
    stay.

Right towards the lamb she look'd ; and from that
    shady place
I unobserved could see the workings of her face ;
If nature to her tongue could measured numbers
    bring,
Thus, thought I, to her lamb that little maid might
    sing :   20

'What ails thee, Young one ? what ? Why pull so
    at thy cord ?
'Is it not well with thee ? well both for bed and
    board ?
'Thy plot of grass is soft, and green as grass can be;
'Rest, little Young one, rest ; what is 't that aileth
    thee ?
        19 If she could write verse

'What is it thou wouldst seek? What is wanting to
thy heart? 25
'Thy limbs are they not strong? and beautiful thou
art!
'This grass is tender grass; these flowers they have
no peers;
'And that green corn all day is rustling in thy ears.

'If the sun be shining hot, do but stretch thy
woollen chain;
'This beech is standing by, its covert thou canst
gain; 30
'For rain and mountain-storms!—the like thou
need'st not fear,
'The rain and storm are things that scarcely can
come here.

'Rest, little Young one, rest; thou hast forgot the
day
'When my father found thee first in places far
away;
'Many flocks were on the hills, but thou wert own'd
by none, 35
'And thy mother from thy side for evermore was
gone.

'He took thee in his arms, and in pity brought thee
home:
'A blesséd day for thee!—then whither wouldst thou
roam?
'A faithful nurse thou hast; the dam that did thee
yean
'Upon the mountain-tops no kinder could have
been. 40

27 *peers.* equals

'Thou know'st that twice a day I have brought thee
    in this can
'Fresh water from the brook, as clear as ever ran ;
'And twice in the day, when the ground is wet with
    dew,
'I bring thee draughts of milk, warm milk it is and
    new.

'Thy limbs will shortly be twice as stout as they are
    now,   45
'Then I'll yoke thee to my cart like a pony in the
    plough !
'My playmate thou shalt be ; and when the wind is
    cold
'Our hearth shall be thy bed, our house shall be
    thy fold.

'It will not, will not rest !—Poor creature, can it be
'That 'tis thy mother's heart which is working so in
    thee ?   50
'Things that I know not of belike to thee are dear,
'And dreams of things which thou canst neither see
    nor hear.

'Alas, the mountain-tops that look so green and fair!
'I've heard of fearful winds and darkness that come
    there ;
'The little brooks that seem all pastime and all
    play,   55
'When they are angry, roar like lions for their prey.

'Here thou need'st not dread the raven in the sky ;
'Night and day thou art safe,—our cottage is
    hard by.
'Why bleat so after me ? Why pull so at thy
    chain ?
'Sleep—and at break of day I will come to thee
    again !'   60

—As homeward through the lane I went with lazy
    feet,
This song to myself did I oftentimes repeat ;
And it seem'd, as I retraced the ballad line by line,
That but half of it was hers, and one half of it was
    mine.

Again, and once again, did I repeat the song ;   65
'Nay,' said I, 'more than half to the damsel must
    belong !—
'For she look'd with such a look, and she spake
    with such a tone,
'That I almost received her heart into my own.'
                  W. Wordsworth

• 3 •

THE LAMB

LITTLE Lamb, who made thee ?
Dost thou know who made thee ?
Gave thee life, and bade thee feed
By the stream and o'er the mead ;
Gave thee clothing of delight,   5
Softest clothing, woolly, bright ;
Gave thee such a tender voice,
Making all the vales rejoice :
    Little Lamb, who made thee ?
    Dost thou know who made thee ?   10

    Little Lamb, I'll tell thee !
    Little Lamb, I'll tell thee.
He is calléd by thy name,
For He calls Himself a Lamb :—

        63 *retraced*, repeated

He is meek, and He is mild ;   15
He became a little child :
I, a child, and thou, a lamb,
We are calléd by His name.
 Little Lamb, God bless thee;
 Little Lamb, God bless thee. 20

W. Blake

* 4 *

EPITAPH ON A HARE

HERE lies, whom hound did ne'er pursue,
 Nor swifter greyhound follow,
Whose foot ne'er tainted morning dew,
 Nor ear heard huntsman's halloo !

Old Tiney, surliest of his kind,   5
 Who, nursed with tender care,
And to domestic bounds confined,
 Was still a wild Jack-hare.

Though duly from my hand he took
 His pittance every night,   10
He did it with a jealous look,
 And, when he could, would bite.

His diet was of wheaten bread,
 And milk, and oats, and straw ;
Thistles, or lettuces instead,   15
 With sand to scour his maw.

On twigs of hawthorn he regaled,
 On pippin's russet peel ;
And when his juicy salads fail'd
 Sliced carrot pleased him well. 20

5 *tainted*, scented 10 *pittance*, portion 16 to make his food digest

A Turkey carpet was his lawn,
  Whereon he loved to bound,
To skip and gambol like a fawn,
  And swing his rump around.

His frisking was at evening hours,   25
  For then he lost his fear ;
But most before approaching showers,
  Or when a storm drew near.

Eight years and five round-rolling moons
  He thus saw steal away,   30
Dozing out all his idle noons,
  And every night at play.

I kept him for his humour's sake,
  For he would oft beguile
My heart of thoughts that made it ache,   35
  And force me to a smile.

But now, beneath this walnut shade,
  He finds his long last home,
And waits, in snug concealment laid,
  Till gentler Puss shall come.   40

He, still more aged, feels the shocks
  From which no care can save :—
And, partner once of Tiney's box,
  Must soon partake his grave.

                              W. Cowper

* 5 *

THE WOUNDED HARE

INHUMAN man ! curse on thy barbarous art,
  And blasted be thy murder-aiming eye ;
  May never pity soothe thee with a sigh,
Nor ever pleasure glad thy cruel heart !

29 *moons*, months   34 *beguile*, cheat
1 *inhuman*, cruel ; *barbarous art*, shooting for sport's sake

—Go, live, poor wanderer of the wood and field, 5
   The bitter little that of life remains ;
   No more the thickening brakes and verdant plains
To thee shall home, or food, or pastime yield.

Seek, mangled wretch, some place of wonted rest,
   No more of rest, but now thy dying bed !   10
   The sheltering rushes whistling o'er thy head,
The cold earth with thy bloody bosom prest.

Oft as by winding Nith, I, musing, wait
   The sober eve, or hail the cheerful dawn,
   I'll miss thee sporting o'er the dewy lawn,   15
And curse the ruffian's aim, and mourn thy hapless
     fate.   *R. Burns*

• 6 •

TO A SPANIEL ON HIS KILLING A YOUNG BIRD

A SPANIEL, Beau, that fares like you,
   Well fed, and at his ease,
Should wiser be than to pursue
   Each trifle that he sees.

But you have kill'd a tiny bird,   5
   Which flew not till to-day,
Against my orders, whom you heard
   Forbidding you the prey.

Nor did you kill that you might eat,
   And ease a doggish pain,   10
For him, though chased with furious heat,
   You left where he was slain.

9 *wonted*, where he had been before   13 *Nith*, river in Ayrshire
    7 *thickening*, growing leafier

Nor was he of the thievish sort,
  Or one whom blood allures,
But innocent was all his sport   15
  Whom you have torn for yours.

My dog ! what remedy remains,
  Since, teach you all I can,
I see you after all my pains
  So much resemble man ?   20

Beau's Reply

Sir, when I flew to seize the bird
  In spite of your command,
A louder voice than yours I heard,
  And harder to withstand.

You cried—forbear !—but in my breast   25
  A mightier cried—proceed !
'Twas Nature, Sir, whose strong behest
  Impell'd me to the deed.

Yet, much as Nature I respect,
  I ventured once to break   30
(As you, perhaps, may recollect)
  Her precept for your sake ;

And when your linnet, on a day,
  Passing his prison door,
Had flutter'd all his strength away,   35
  And, panting, press'd the floor ;

Well knowing him a sacred thing,
  Not destined to my tooth,
I only kiss'd his ruffled wing,
  And lick'd the feathers smooth.   40

14 *allures*, tempts   17 *remedy*, cure   27 *behest*, command
28 *impell'd*, drove   32 *precept*, order   38 *destined*, meant for

Let my obedience then excuse
    My disobedience now,
Nor some reproof yourself refuse
    From your aggrieved Bow-wow ;

If killing birds be such a crime   45
    (Which I can hardly see),
What think you, Sir, of *killing time*,
    With verse address'd to me ?

                                        W. Cowper

* 7 *

THE BLIND BOY

O SAY what is that thing call'd Light,
    Which I must ne'er enjoy ;
What are the blessings of the Sight :
    O tell your poor blind boy !

You talk of wondrous things you see ;   5
    You say the sun shines bright ;
I feel him warm, but how can he
    Or make it day or night ?

My day or night myself I make
    Whene'er I sleep or play ;   10
And could I ever keep awake
    With me 'twere always day.

With heavy sighs I often hear
    You mourn my hapless woe ;
But sure with patience I can bear   15
    A loss I ne'er can know.

Then let not what I cannot have
    My cheer of mind destroy :
Whilst thus I sing, I am a king,
    Although a poor blind boy.   20

                                        C. Cibber

44 *aggrieved*, vexed   47 *killing*, wasting   14 *hapless*, unhappy

* 8 *

ALICE FELL

THE post-boy drove with fierce career,
For threatening clouds the moon had drown'd ;
When, as we hurried on, my ear
Was smitten with a startling sound.

As if the wind blew many ways,   5
I heard the sound,—and more and more ;
It seem'd to follow with the chaise,
And still I heard it as before.

At length I to the boy call'd out ;
He stopp'd his horses at the word,   10
But neither cry, nor voice, nor shout,
Nor aught else like it, could be heard.

The boy then smack'd his whip, and fast
The horses scamper'd through the rain ;
But hearing soon upon the blast   15
The cry, I bade him halt again.

Forthwith alighting on the ground,
'Whence comes,' said I, 'this piteous moan ?'
And there a little girl I found,
Sitting behind the chaise alone.   20

' My cloak !' no other word she spake,
But loud and bitterly she wept,
As if her innocent heart would break ;
And down from off her seat she leapt.

'What ails you, child ?'—she sobb'd, 'Look
        here !'   25
I saw it in the wheel entangled,
A weather-beaten rag as e'er
From any garden scarecrow dangled.

There, twisted between nave and spoke,
It hung, nor could at once be freed ;   30
But our joint pains unloosed the cloak,
A miserable rag indeed !

'And whither are you going, child,
'To-night, along these lonesome ways?'
'To Durham,' answer'd she, half wild—   35
'Then come with me into the chaise.'

Insensible to all relief
Sat the poor girl, and forth did send
Sob after sob, as if her grief
Could never, never have an end.   40

'My child, in Durham do you dwell?'
She check'd herself in her distress,
And said, 'My name is Alice Fell ;
'I'm fatherless and motherless.

'And I to Durham, Sir, belong.'   45
Again, as if the thought would choke
Her very heart, her grief grew strong ;
And all was for her tatter'd cloak.

The chaise drove on ; our journey's end
Was nigh ; and, sitting by my side,   50
As if she had lost her only friend,
She wept, nor would be pacified.

Up to the tavern-door we post :
Of Alice and her grief I told,
And I gave money to the host,   55
To buy a new cloak for the old.

'And let it be of duffil gray,
'As warm a cloak as man can sell !'
—Proud creature was she the next day,
The little orphan, Alice Fell !   60

W. Wordsworth

52 *pacified*, quieted   57 *duffil*, strong shaggy cloth

• 9 •

THE LITTLE GIRL LOST

IN the southern clime,
Where the summer's prime
Never fades away,
Lovely Lyca lay.

Seven summers old   5
Lovely Lyca told ;
She had wander'd long,
Hearing wild-birds' song.

' Sweet sleep, come to me
' Underneath this tree !   10
' Do father, mother, weep ?
' Where can Lyca sleep ?

' Lost in desert wild
' Is your little child !
' How can Lyca sleep   15
' If her mother weep ?

' If her heart does ache
' Then let Lyca wake :—
' If my mother sleep,
' Lyca shall not weep.   20

' Frowning, frowning, night
' O'er this desert bright,
' Let thy moon arise
' While I close my eyes !'

Sleeping Lyca lay :   25
While the beasts of prey
Come from caverns deep,
View'd the maid asleep.

The kingly lion stood,
And the virgin view'd :   30
Then he gamboll'd round
O'er the hallow'd ground.

Leopards, tigers, play
Round her as she lay ;
While the lion old   35
Bow'd his mane of gold,

And [did] her bosom lick ;
And upon her neck
From his eyes of flame
Ruby tears there came :   40

While the lioness
Loosed her slender dress ;
And naked they convey'd
To caves the sleeping maid.

THE LITTLE GIRL FOUND

ALL the night in woe
Lyca's parents go,
Over valleys deep,
While the deserts weep.

Tired and woe-begone,   5
Hoarse with making moan,
Arm-in-arm seven days
They traced the desert ways.

Seven nights they sleep
Among shadows deep,   10
And dream they see their child
Starved in desert wild.

Pale through pathless ways
The fancied image strays,
Famish'd, weeping, weak,   15
With hollow piteous shriek

Rising from unrest
The trembling woman press'd
With feet of weary woe :
She could no further go.   20

In his arms he bore
Her, arm'd with sorrow sore ;
Till before their way
A couching lion lay.

Turning back was vain :   25
Soon his heavy mane
Bore them to the ground ;
Then he stalk'd around

Smelling to his prey ;
But their fears allay,   30
When he licks their hands,
And silent by them stands.

They look upon his eyes,
Fill'd with deep surprise ;
And wondering behold   35
A spirit arm'd in gold.

On his head a crown :
On his shoulders down
Flow'd his golden hair !
Gone was all their care.   40

'Follow me,' he said ;
'Weep not for the maid ;
'In my palace deep
'Lyca lies asleep.'

Then they followéd   45
Where the vision led,
And saw their sleeping child
Among tigers wild.

To this day they dwell
In a lonely dell ;   50
Nor fear the wolvish howl,
Nor the lions' growl.

W Blake

* IO *

JOHN GILPIN

JOHN Gilpin was a citizen
  Of credit and renown,
A train-band captain eke was he
  Of famous London Town.

John Gilpin's spouse said to her dear,   5
  'Though wedded we have been
'These twice ten tedious years, yet we
  'No holiday have seen.

'To-morrow is our wedding-day,
  'And we will then repair   10
'Unto the Bell at Edmonton,
  'All in a chaise and pair.

'My sister and my sister's child,
  'Myself, and children three,
'Will fill the chaise ; so you must ride   15
  'On horseback after we.'

He soon replied, 'I do admire
  'Of womankind but one,
'And you are she, my dearest dear,
  'Therefore it shall be done.   20

train-band, militia

'I am a linendraper bold,
　'As all the world doth know,
'And my good friend, the Calender,
　'Will lend his horse to go.'

Quoth Mistress Gilpin, 'That's well said ;　25
　'And, for that wine is dear,
'We will be furnish'd with our own,
　· 'Which is both bright and clear.'

John Gilpin kiss'd his loving wife ;
　O'erjoy'd was he to find　　　　30
That, though on pleasure she was bent,
　She had a frugal mind.

The morning came, the chaise was brought,
　But yet was not allow'd
To drive up to the door, lest all　　35
　Should say that she was proud.

So three doors off the chaise was stay'd,
　Where they did all get in,
Six precious souls, and all agog
　To dash through thick and thin.　40

Smack went the whip, round went the wheels ;
　Were never folks so glad :
The stones did rattle underneath,
　As if Cheapside were mad.

John Gilpin, at his horse's side,　　45
　Seized fast the flowing mane,
And up he got, in haste to ride,
　But soon came down again ;

For saddle-tree scarce reach'd had he,
　His journey to begin,　　　　50
When, turning round his head, he saw
　Three customers come in.

23 *Calender*, cloth-dresser　　44 a street in London
　49 *saddle-tree*, bow of the saddle

So down he came ; for loss of time
    Although it grieved him sore,
Yet loss of pence, full well he knew,   55
    Would trouble him much more.

'Twas long before the customers
    Were suited to their mind,
When Betty, screaming, came downstairs,
    ' The wine is left behind ! '   60

' Good lack ! ' quoth he, ' yet bring it me,
    ' My leathern belt likewise,
' In which I bear my trusty sword
    ' When I do exercise.'

Now Mistress Gilpin (careful soul !)   65
    Had two stone-bottles found,
To hold the liquor that she loved,
    And keep it safe and sound.

Each bottle had a curling ear,
    Through which the belt he drew,   70
And hung a bottle on each side,
    To make his balance true.

Then over all, that he might be
    Equipp'd from top to toe,
His long red cloak, well-brush'd and neat,   75
    He manfully did throw.

Now see him mounted once again
    Upon his nimble steed,
Full slowly pacing o'er the stones,
    With caution and good heed.   80

But finding soon a smoother road
    Beneath his well-shod feet,
The snorting beast began to trot,
    Which gall'd him in his seat.

64 as a soldier   74 *equipp'd*, dressed out

So, 'Fair and softly!' John he cried,   85
 But John he cried in vain ;
That trot became a gallop soon,
 In spite of curb and rein.

So stooping down, as needs he must
 Who cannot sit upright,   90
He grasp'd the mane with both his hands,
 And eke with all his might.

His horse, who never in that sort
 Had handled been before,
What thing upon his back had got   95
 Did wonder more and more.

Away went Gilpin, neck or nought ;
 Away went hat and wig ;
He little dreamt, when he set out,
 Of running such a rig.   100

The wind did blow, the cloak did fly,
 Like streamer long and gay,
Till loop and button failing both,
 At last it flew away.

Then might all people well discern   105
 The bottles he had slung ;
A bottle swinging at each side,
 As hath been said or sung.

The dogs did bark, the children scream'd,
 Up flew the windows all ;   110
And every soul cried out—'Well done !'
 As loud as he could bawl.

Away went Gilpin—who but he ?
 His fame soon spread around,
'He carries weight ; he rides a race !   115
 ''Tis for a thousand pound !'

92 *eke*, also

And still as fast as he drew near,
  'Twas wonderful to view
How in a trice the turnpike men
  Their gates wide open threw.   120

And now, as he went bowing down
  His reeking head full low,
The bottles twain behind his back
  Were shatter'd at a blow.

Down ran the wine into the road,   125
  Most piteous to be seen,
Which made his horse's flanks to smoke
  As they had basted been.

But still he seem'd to carry weight,
  With leathern girdle braced ;   130
For all might see the bottle-necks
  Still dangling at his waist.

Thus all through merry Islington
  These gambols he did play,
Until he came unto the Wash   135
  Of Edmonton so gay ;

And there he threw the Wash about
  On both sides of the way,
Just like unto a trundling mop,
  Or a wild goose at play.   140

At Edmonton his loving wife
  From the balcóny spied
Her tender husband, wondering much
  To see how he did ride.

'Stop, stop, John Gilpin !—Here's the house'— 145
  They all at once did cry ;
'The dinner waits, and we are tired ;'
  Said Gilpin, 'So am I !'

119 *trice* moment   122 *reeking*, steaming   128 with gravy

But yet his horse was not a whit
   Inclined to tarry there ;   150
For why? his owner had a house
   Full ten miles off, at Ware.

So like an arrow swift he flew,
   Shot by an archer strong ;
So did he fly—which brings me to   155
   The middle of my song.

Away went Gilpin, out of breath,
   And sore against his will,
Till at his friend the Calender's
   His horse at last stood still.   160

The Calender, amazed to see
   His neighbour in such trim,
Laid down his pipe, flew to the gate,
   And thus accosted him.

'What news? what news? your tidings tell ! 165
   'Tell me you must and shall —
'Say, why bare-headed you are come,
   'Or why you come at all?'

Now Gilpin had a pleasant wit,
   And loved a timely joke ;   170
And thus unto the Calender
   In merry guise he spoke :

'I came, because your horse would come ;
   'And, if I well forbode,
'My hat and wig will soon be here,   175
   'They are upon the road.'

The Calender, right glad to find
   His friend in merry pin,
Return'd him not a single word,
   But to the house went in ;   180

149 *whit*, bit   164 *accosted*, spoke to   174 *forbode*, prophecy
178 *pin*, humour

Whence straight he came, with hat and wig,
  A wig that flow'd behind ;
A hat not much the worse for wear ;
  Each comely in its kind.

He held them up, and in his turn   185
  Thus show'd his ready wit :
' My head is twice as big as yours,
  ' They therefore needs must fit.

' But let me scrape the dirt away,
  ' That hangs upon your face ;   190
' And stop and eat, for well you may
  ' Be in a hungry case.'

Said John, ' It is my wedding-day,
  ' And all the world would stare,
' If wife should dine at Edmonton,   195
  'And I should dine at Ware !'

So, turning to his horse, he said,
  ' I am in haste to dine ;
''Twas for your pleasure you came here,
  'You shall go back for mine.'   200

Ah, luckless speech, and bootless boast !
  For which he paid full dear ;
For, while he spake, a braying ass
  Did sing most loud and clear ;

Whereat his horse did snort, as he   205
  Had heard a lion roar,
And gallop'd off with all his might,
  As he had done before.

Away went Gilpin, and away
  Went Gilpin's hat and wig :   210
He lost them sooner than at first,
  For why?—they were too big.

201 *bootless*, vain

Now Mistress Gilpin, when she saw
  Her husband posting down
Into the country far away,   215
  She pull'd out half-a-crown ;

And thus unto the youth she said,
  That drove them to the Bell,
'This shall be yours, when you bring back
  ' My husband safe and well.'   220

The youth did ride, and soon did meet
  John coming back amain ;
Whom in a trice he tried to stop,
  By catching at his rein ;

But not performing what he meant,   225
  And gladly would have done,
The frighten'd steed he frighten'd more,
  And made him faster run.

Away went Gilpin, and away
  Went postboy at his heels,   230
The postboy's horse right glad to miss
  The lumbering of the wheels.

Six gentlemen upon the road
  Thus seeing Gilpin fly,
With postboy scampering in the rear,   235
  They raised the hue and cry:—

' Stop thief !—stop thief !—a highwayman !'
  Not one of them was mute ;
And all and each that pass'd that way
  Did join in the pursuit.   240

And now the turnpike gates again
  Flew open in short space:
The toll-men thinking as before
  That Gilpin rode a race.

And so he did, and won it too !   245
   For he got first to town ;
Nor stopp'd, till where he had got up
   He did again get down.

— Now let us sing, Long live the King,
   And Gilpin, long live he ;   250
And, when he next doth ride abroad,
   May I be there to see !

                            W. Cowper

* I I *

WILLIAM AND MARGARET

'TWAS at the silent, solemn hour
   When night and morning meet ;
In glided Margaret's grimly ghost,
   And stood at William's feet.

Her face was like an April morn,   5
   Clad in a wintry cloud ;
And clay-cold was her lily hand,
   That held her sable shroud.

So shall the fairest face appear
   When youth and years are flown :   10
Such is the robe that kings must wear,
   When death has reft their crown.

Her bloom was like the springing flower,
   That sips the silver dew ;
The rose was budded in her cheek,   15
   Just opening to the view.

But love had, like the cankerworm,
   Consumed her early prime:
The rose grew pale, and left her cheek ;
   She died before her time.   20

            12 *reft*, taken

'Awake !' she cried, 'thy true Love calls,
  'Come from her midnight grave ;
'Now let thy pity hear the maid,
  'Thy love refused to save !

'This is the dumb and dreary hour,   25
  'When injured ghosts complain ;
'When yawning graves give up their dead,
  'To haunt the faithless swain.

'Bethink thee, William, of thy fault,
  'Thy pledge and broken oath !   30
'And give me back my maiden-vow,
  'And give me back my troth.

'Why did you promise love to me,
  'And not that promise keep?
'Why did you swear my eyes were bright,   35
  'Yet leave those eyes to weep ?

'How could you say my face was fair,
  'And yet that face forsake ?
'How could you win my virgin heart,
  'Yet leave that heart to break ?   40

'Why did you say my lip was sweet,
  'And made the scarlet pale ?
'And why did I, young witless maid :
  'Believe the flattering tale ?

'That face, alas ! no more is fair,   45
  'Those lips no longer red :
'Dark are my eyes, now closed in death,
  'And every charm is fled.

'The hungry worm my sister is ;
  'This winding-sheet I wear :   50
'And cold and weary lasts our night,
  'Till that last morn appear.

28 *swain*, lover   32 *troth*, promise   48 *charm*, beauty

'But, hark! the cock has warn'd me hence;
    'A long and late adieu!
'Come see, false man, how low she lies   55
    'Who died for love of you!'

The lark sung loud; the morning smiled
    With beams of rosy red:
Pale William quaked in every limb,
    And raving left his bed.   60

He hied him to the fatal place
    Where Margaret's body lay;
And stretch'd him on the green-grass turf
    That wrapp'd her breathless clay.

And thrice he call'd on Margaret's name,   65
    And thrice he wept full sore;
Then laid his cheek to her cold grave,
    And word spake never more!

                                   D. Mallet

* I 2 *

THE TRUE SWEETHEART

A FAIR maid sat at her bower-door,
    Wringing her lily hands;
And by it came a sprightly youth
    Fast tripping o'er the strands.

'Where gang ye, young John,' she says,   5
    'Sae early in the day?
'It gars me think, by your fast trip,
    'Your journey's far away.'

He turn'd about with surly look,
    And said, 'What's that to thee?   10
'I'm gaen' to see a lovely maid
    'Mair fairer far than ye.'

54 *adieu*, good-bye   5 *gang*, go   7 *gars*, makes   12 *mair*. more

—'False Love, and hast thou play'd me this
  'In summer among the flowers?
'I will repay thee back again   15
  'In winter among the showers.

'Unless again, again, my Love,
  'Unless you turn again;
'As you with other maidens rove,
  'I'll smile on other men.'   20

—'O make your choice of whom you please,
  'For I my choice will have;
'I've chosen a maid mair fair than thee,
  'I never will deceive.'

She kilted up her clothing fine,   25
  And after him gaed she;
But aye he said, 'Turn back, turn back,
  'No further gang with me!'

'—But again, dear Love, and again, dear Love,
  'Will ye ne'er love me again?   30
'Alas for loving you sae weel,
  'And you nae me again!'

The firstan town that they came till,
  He bought her brooch and ring;
But aye he bade her turn again,   35
  And no farther gang with him.

' But again, dear Love, and again, dear Love,
  'Will ye ne'er love me again?
'Alas! for loving you sae weel,
  'And you nae me again!'   40

The second town that they came till,
  His heart it grew more fain;
And he was as deep in love with her
  As she with him again.

25 *kilted*, tucked   31 *sae weel*, so well   33 *firstan*, first; *till*, to

The neistan town that they came till,   45
   He bought her wedding-gown ;
And made her lady of halls and bowers,
   In bonny Berwick town.

Unknown

* 13 ·*

THE GAY GOSHAWK

'O WELL is me, my gay goshawk,
   'That you can speak and flee ;
'For you can carry a love-letter
   'To my true Love from me.'

—'O how can I carry a letter to her ?   5
   'Or how should I her know ?
'I bear a tongue ne'er with her spake,
   'And eyes that ne'er her saw.'

—'O well shall ye my true Love ken
   'So soon as ye her see :   10
'For of all the flowers of fair England,
   'The fairest flower is she.

'And when she goes into the house,
   'Sit ye upon the whin ;
'And sit you there and sing our loves   15
   'As she goes out and in.'

Lord William has written a love-letter,
   Put it under his pinion gray :
And he's awa' to Southern land
   As fast as wings can gae.   20

And first he sang a low, low, note,
   And then he sang a clear ;
And aye the o'erword of the sang
   Was 'Your Love can no win here.'

---

45 *neistan*, next   1 *goshawk*, large hawk   14 *whin*, furze-bush
   23 *o'erword*, burden   24 *no win*, not come

'Feast on, feast on, my maidens all,   25
  'The wine flows you amang ;
'While I gang to my shot-window
  'And hear yon bonnie bird's sang.'

O, first he sang a merry sang,
  And then he sang a grave :   30
And then he peck'd his feathers gray ;
  To her the letter gave.

'Have there a letter from Lord William :
  'He says, he sent ye three ;
'He can not wait your love longer,   35
  'But for your sake he'll die.'

—'I send him the rings from my white fingers,
  'The garlands of my hair ;
'I send him the heart that's in my breast ;
  'What would my Love have mair ?   40
'And at Mary's kirk in fair Scotland,
  'Ye'll bid him wait for me there.'

She hied her to her father dear
  As fast as go could she :
'An asking, an asking, my father dear,   45
  'An asking grant you me !
'That if I die in fair England,
  'In Scotland bury me.

'At the first kirk of fair Scotland,
  'You cause the bells be rung ;   50
'At the second kirk of fair Scotland,
  'You cause the mass be sung ;

'And when ye come to Saint Mary's kirk,
  'Ye'll tarry there till night.'
And so her father pledged his word,   55
  And so his promise plight.

27 *shot-window*, window with shutter   41 *kirk*, church
      52 *mass*, service   56 *plight*, gave

The lady's gone to her chamber
  As fast as she could fare ;
And she has drunk a sleepy draught
  That she had mix'd with care.   60

And pale, pale, grew her rosy cheek,
  And pale and cold was she :—
She seem'd to be as surely dead
  As any corpse could be.

Then spake her cruel stepminnie,   65
  ' Take ye the burning lead,
' And drop a drop on her bosom,
  ' To try if she be dead.'

They dropp'd the hot lead on her cheek,
  They dropp'd it on her chin,   70
They dropp'd it on her bosom white ;
  But she spake none again.

Then up arose her seven brethren,
  And hew'd to her a bier ;
They hew'd it from the solid oak ;   75
  Laid it o'er with silver clear.

The first Scots kirk that they came to
  They gart the bells be rung ;
The next Scots kirk that they came to
  They gart the mass be sung.   80

But when they came to Saint Mary's kirk,
  There stood spearmen in a row ;
And up and started Lord William,
  The chieftain among them a'.

He rent the sheet upon her face   85
  A little above her chin :
With rosy cheek, and ruby lip,
  She look'd and laugh'd to him.

—'A morsel of your bread, my lord !
  'And one glass of your wine !   90
'For I have fasted these three long days
  'All for your sake and mine !'

Unknown

* 14 *

THE MARINERS OF ENGLAND

YE Mariners of England
That guard our native seas !
Whose flag has braved, a thousand years,
The battle and the breeze !
Your glorious standard launch again   5
To match another foe :
And sweep through the deep,
While the stormy winds do blow ;
While the battle rages loud and long
And the stormy winds do blow.   10

The spirits of your fathers
Shall start from every wave—
For the deck it was their field of fame,
And Ocean was their grave :
Where Blake and mighty Nelson fell   15
Your manly hearts shall glow,
As ye sweep through the deep,
While the stormy winds do blow ;
While the battle rages loud and long
And the stormy winds do blow.   20

Britannia needs no bulwarks,
No towers along the steep ;
Her march is o'er the mountain waves,
Her home is on the deep.
With thunders from her native oak   25
She quells the floods below—

5 *standard*, flag of England   15 *Blake*, admiral under the Commonwealth   21 Our island needs no coast fortifications

As they roar on the shore,
When the stormy winds do blow ;
When the battle rages loud and long,
And the stormy winds do blow.   30

The meteor-flag of England
Shall yet terrific burn ;
Till danger's troubled night depart
And the star of peace return.
Then, then, ye ocean-warriors !   35
Our song and feast shall flow
To the fame of your name,
When the storm has ceased to blow ;
When the fiery fight is heard no more,
And the storm has ceased to blow.

T. Campbell

* 15 *

BEFORE BATTLE

THE signal to engage shall be
    A whistle and a hollo ;
Be one and all but firm, like me,
    And conquest soon will follow !
You, Gunnel, keep the helm in hand—   5
    Thus, thus, boys ! steady, steady
Till right a-head you see the land,—
    Then soon as we are ready,
        —The signal to engage shall be
            A whistle and a hollo ;   10
        Be one and all but firm, like me,
            And conquest soon will follow !

Keep, boys, a good look out, d'ye hear ?
    'Tis for Old England's honour ;
Just as you brought your lower tier   15
    Broad-side to bear upon her,

---

31 *meteor-flag*, streaming like a flying star   15 *tier*, a row of cannon
16 *bear upon*, be pointed towards

—The signal to engage shall be
  A whistle and a hollo;
Be one and all but firm, like me,
  And conquest soon will follow! 20

All hands then, lads, the ship to clear;
  Load all your guns and mortars;
Silent as death th' attack prepare;
  And, when you're all at quarters,
    —The signal to engage shall be 25
      A whistle and a hollo;
    Be one and all but firm, like me,
      And conquest soon will follow!

                  C. Dibdin

⁎ 16 ⁎

CASABIANCA

A True Story

THE boy stood on the burning deck,
  Whence all but he had fled;
The flame that lit the battle's wreck,
  Shone round him o'er the dead;
Yet beautiful and bright he stood 5
  As born to rule the storm!
A creature of heroic blood,
  A proud, though child-like form!

The flames roll'd on—he would not go
  Without his Father's word; 10
That Father, faint in death below,
  His voice no longer heard.
He call'd aloud: 'Say, father, say
  'If yet my task is done!'
He knew not that the chieftain lay 15
  Unconscious of his son.

---

22 *mortars,* guns to shoot bombs   **7** *heroic,* noble   **15** *chieftain,*
admiral in command

'Speak, father!' once again he cried,
  'If I may yet be gone!'
And but the booming shots replied,
  And fast the flames roll'd on.   20
Upon his brow he felt their breath,
  And in his waving hair;
And look'd from that lone post of death
  In still, yet brave despair;

And shouted but once more aloud,   25
  'My father! must I stay?'
While o'er him fast through sail and shroud,
  The wreathing fires made way.
They wrapt the ship in splendour wild,
  They caught the flag on high,   30
And stream'd above the gallant child
  Like banners in the sky.

There came a burst of thunder-sound—
  The boy—O! where was he?
—Ask of the winds that far around   35
  With fragments strew'd the sea,
With mast, and helm, and pennon fair,
  That well had borne their part;
But the noblest thing which perish'd there
  Was that young faithful heart!   40
               F. Hemans

* 17 *

THE LOSS OF THE BIRKENHEAD:

Supposed to be told by a Soldier who survived

RIGHT on our flank the crimson sun went down;
The deep sea roll'd around in dark repose;
When, like the wild shriek from some captured
    town,
  A cry of women rose.

19 *but*, only: *booming*, deep sounding   37 *pennon*, small flag
1 *flank*, side 3 *captured*, taken in war

The stout ship Birkenhead lay hard and fast,   5
Caught without hope upon a hidden rock ;
Her timbers thrill'd as nerves, when through them
       pass'd
    The spirit of that shock.

And ever like base cowards, who leave their ranks
In danger's hour, before the rush of steel,   10
Drifted away disorderly the planks
    From underneath her keel.

So calm the air, so calm and still the flood,
That low down in its blue translucent glass
We saw the great fierce fish, that thirst for blood,   15
    Pass slowly, then repass.

They tarried, the waves tarried, for their prey !
The sea turn'd one clear smile ! Like things asleep
Those dark shapes in the azure silence lay,
    As quiet as the deep.   20

Then amidst oath, and prayer, and rush, and wreck,
Faint screams, faint questions waiting no reply,
Our Colonel gave the word, and on the deck
    Form'd us in line to die.

To die !—'twas hard, whilst the sleek ocean glow'd 25
Beneath a sky as fair as summer flowers :—
All to the boats ! cried one :—he was, thank God,
    No officer of ours !

Our English hearts beat true :—we would not stir :
That base appeal we heard, but heeded not :   30
On land, on sea, we had our Colours, Sir,
    To keep without a spot !

They shall not say in England, that we fought
With shameful strength, unhonour'd life to seek ;
Into mean safety, mean deserters, brought   35
    By trampling down the weak.

10 *rush of steel,* battle 14 *translucent,* transparent 15 *fish,* sharks

So we made women with their children go,
The oars ply back again, and yet again ;
Whilst, inch by inch, the drowning ship sank low,
    Still under steadfast men.   40

—What follows, why recall ?—The brave who died,
Died without flinching in the bloody surf,
They sleep as well, beneath that purple tide,
    As others under turf :—

They sleep as well ! and, roused from their wild
    grave,   45
Wearing their wounds like stars, shall rise again,
Joint-heirs with Christ, because they bled to save
    His weak ones, not in vain.
                Sir F. H. Doyle

* 18 *

THE 'NORTHERN STAR'

A Tynemouth Ship

The ' Northern Star '
Sail'd over the bar
Bound to the Baltic Sea ;
In the morning gray
She stretch'd away :—   5
'Twas a weary day to me !

For many an hour
In sleet and shower
By the lighthouse rock I stray ;
And watch till dark   10
For the wingèd bark
Of him that is far away.

The castle's bound
I wander round,
Amidst the grassy graves :   15

11 *wingèd*, with sails   15 Tynemouth Castle, used as a graveyard

But all I hear
  Is the north-wind drear,
And all I see are the waves.

  The ' Northern Star'
  Is set afar !   20
Set in the Baltic Sea :
  And the waves have spread
  The sandy bed
That holds my Love from me.

Unknown.

* 19 *

THE OFFICER'S GRAVE

THERE is in the wide, lone sea
  A spot unmark'd but holy ;
For there the gallant and the free
  In his ocean-bed lies lowly.

Down, down, within the deep   5
  That oft to triumph bore him,
He sleeps a sound and pleasant sleep
  With the salt waves dashing o'er him.

He sleeps serene and safe
  From tempest or from billow,   10
Where the storms that high above him chafe
  Scarce rock his peaceful pillow.

The sea and him in death
  They did not dare to sever :
It was his home while he had breath :   15
  'Tis now his rest for ever !

Sleep on, thou mighty dead !
  A glorious tomb they've found thee ;
The broad blue sky above thee spread :
  The boundless waters round thee.   20

H. F. Lyte

* 20 *

LOSS OF THE ROYAL GEORGE

TOLL for the Brave !
The brave that are no more !
All sunk beneath the wave
Fast by their native shore !

Eight hundred of the brave
Whose courage well was tried,
Had made the vessel heel
And laid her on her side.

A land-breeze shook the shrouds
And she was overset ;   10
Down went the Royal George,
With all her crew complete.

Toll for the brave !
Brave Kempenfelt is gone ;
His last sea-fight is fought,   15
His work of glory done.

It was not in the battle ;
No tempest gave the shock ;
She sprang no fatal leak,
She ran upon no rock.   20

His sword was in its sheath.
His fingers held the pen,
When Kempenfelt went down.
With twice four hundred men.

—Weigh the vessel up   25
Once dreaded by our foes !
And mingle with our cup
The tears that England owes.

7 *heel,* lean over   9 *shrouds,* mast ropes   19 *sprang,* opened
25 *weigh* lift   27 *cup,* rejoicing

Her timbers yet are sound,
And she may float again 30
Full charged with England's thunder,
And plough the distant main :

But Kempenfelt is gone,
His victories are o'er ;
And he and his eight hundred 35
Shall plough the wave no more.

W. Cowper

* 21 *

THE SAILOR'S WIFE

AND are ye sure the news is true ?
And are ye sure he's weel ?
Is this a time to think o' wark ?
Ye jades, lay by your wheel ;
Is this the time to spin a thread, 5
When Colin's at the door ?
Reach down my cloak, I'll to the quay,
And see him come ashore.
    For there's nae luck about the house,
      There's nae luck at a' ; 10
    There's little pleasure in the house
      When our gudeman's awa'.

And gie to me my bigonet,
My bishop's satin gown ;
For I maun tell the bailie's wife 15
That Colin's in the town.
My Turkey slippers maun gae on,
My stockin's pearly blue ;
It's a' to pleasure our gudeman,
For he's baith leal and true. 20

31 *thunder*, cannon   2 *weel*, well   4 *jades*, girls   10 *at a'*, at all
12 *gudeman*, master of the house   13 *bigonet*, little cap   15 *maun*,
must : *bailie*, magistrate   20 *leal*, faithful

Rise, lass, and mak a clean fireside,
   Put on the muckle pot ;
Gie little Kate her button gown
   And Jock his Sunday coat ;
And mak their shoon as black as slaes,   25
   Their hose as white as snaw ;
It's a' to please my ain gudeman,
   For he's been long awa'.

There's twa fat hens upo' the coop
   Been fed this month and mair ;   30
Mak haste and thraw their necks about,
   That Colin weel may fare ;
And spread the table neat and clean,
   Gar ilka thing look braw,
For wha can tell how Colin fared   35
   When he was far awa'?

Sae true his heart, sae smooth his speech,
   His breath like caller air ;
His very foot has music in 't
   As he comes up the stair :—   40
And will I see his face again ?
   And will I hear him speak ?
I'm downright dizzy wi' the thought,
   In troth I'm like to greet.

If Colin's weel, and weel content,   45
   I hae nae mair to crave,
And gin I live to keep him sae,
   I'm blest aboon the lave :
And will I see his face again,
   And will I hear him speak ?   50
I'm downright dizzy wi' the thought,
   In troth I'm like to greet.

---

22 *muckle*, big 25 *slaes*, sloes 31 *thraw*, twist 34 *gar*, make:
ilka, every: *braw*, smart 38 *caller*, fresh 44 *greet*, cry 47 *gin*, if
    48 *aboon the lave*, beyond every one else

For there's nae luck about the house,
   There's nae luck at a' ;
There's little pleasure in the house   55
   When our gudeman's awa'.

W. J. Mickle

* 22 *

A SEA DIRGE

FULL fathom five thy father lies :
   Of his bones are coral made ;
Those are pearls that were his eyes :
   Nothing of him that doth fade,
But doth suffer a sea-change   5
Into something rich and strange ;
Sea-nymphs hourly ring his knell :
Hark ! now I hear them—
   Ding, Dong, Bell.

W. Shakespeare

* 23 *

A LAND DIRGE

CALL for the robin-redbreast and the wren,
   Since o'er shady groves they hover,
   And with leaves and flowers do cover
The friendless bodies of unburied men.
   Call unto his funeral dole   5
   The ant, the field-mouse, and the mole
To rear him hillocks that shall keep him warm,
And (when gay tombs are robb'd) sustain no harm:
But keep the wolf far thence, that's foe to men :
For with his nails he'll dig them up again.   10

J. Webster

---

1 Full five fathoms under water 7 *sea-nymphs*, fairies 8 *gay*,
splendid 5 *dole*, feast

* 24 *

THE SOLITUDE OF ALEXANDER SELKIRK

I AM monarch of all I survey;
    My right there is none to dispute;
From the centre all round to the sea
    I am lord of the fowl and the brute.
O Solitude! where are the charms   5
    That sages have seen in thy face?
Better dwell in the midst of alarms
    Then reign in this horrible place.

I am out of humanity's reach,
    I must finish my journey alone,   10
Never hear the sweet music of speech;
    I start at the sound of my own.
The beasts that roam over the plain
    My form with indifference see;
They are so unacquainted with man,   15
    Their tameness is shocking to me.

Society, Friendship, and Love,
    Divinely bestow'd upon man,
O had I the wings of a dove
    How soon would I taste you again!   20
My sorrows I then might assuage
    In the ways of religion and truth,
Might learn from the wisdom of age,
    And be cheer'd by the sallies of youth.

Ye winds that have made me your sport,   25
    Convey to this desolate shore
Some cordial endearing report
    Of a land I shall visit no more:—
My friends, do they now and then send
    A wish or a thought after me?   30
O tell me I yet have a friend,
    Though a friend I am never to see!

6 *sages*, wise people   9 *humanity*, human creatures   21 *assuage*, heal
24 *sallies*, lively talk   27 *report*, news

How fleet is a glance of the mind !
   Compared with the speed of its flight,
The tempest itself lags behind,   35
   And the swift-wingéd arrows of light.
When I think of my own native land
   In a moment I seem to be there ;
But alas ! recollection at hand
   Soon hurries me back to despair.   40

—But the seafowl is gone to her nest,
   The beast is laid down in his lair ;
Even here is a season of rest,
   And I to my cabin repair.
There's mercy in every place,   45
   And mercy, encouraging thought !
Gives even affliction a grace,
   And reconciles man to his lot.

                        W. Cowper

* 25 *

AT SEA

A WET sheet and a flowing sea,
   A wind that follows fast
And fills the white and rustling sail
   And bends the gallant mast ;
And bends the gallant mast, my boys,   5
   While like the eagle free
Away the good ship flies, and leaves
   Old England on the lee.

O for a soft and gentle wind !
   I heard a fair one cry ;   10
But give to me the snoring breeze
   And white waves heaving high ;

33 *glance*, thought   42 *lair*, den   44 *repair*, go   48 makes us content with life   1 *sheet*, sail-ropes 8 *lee*, behind

And white waves heaving high, my lads,
   The good ship tight and free :—
The world of waters is our home,   15
   And merry men are we.

There's tempest in yon hornéd moon,
   And lightning in yon cloud ;
But hark the music, mariners !
   The wind is piping loud ;   20
The wind is piping loud, my boys,
   The lightning flashes free—
While the hollow oak our palace is,
   Our heritage the sea.

A. Cunningham

* 26 *

SPRING

SPRING, the sweet Spring, is the year's pleasant
      king ;
Then blooms each thing, then maids dance in a
      ring,
Cold doth not sting, the pretty birds do sing,
   Cuckoo, jug-jug, pu-we, to-witta-woo !

The palm and may make country houses gay,   5
Lambs frisk and play, the shepherds pipe all day,
And we hear aye birds tune this merry lay,
   Cuckoo, jug-jug, pu-we, to-witta-woo.

The fields breathe sweet, the daisies kiss our feet,
Young lovers meet, old wives a-sunning sit,   10
In every street these tunes our ears do greet,
   Cuckoo, jug-jug, pu-we, to-witta-woo !
         Spring ! the sweet Spring !

T. Nash

17 *hornéd*, new   23 *oak*, ship   24 *heritage*, proper home

* 27 *

COUNTRY SCENES IN OLD DAYS

Day-break

SEE the day begins to break,
And the light shoots like a streak
Of subtle fire ; the wind blows cold
While the morning doth unfold ;
Now the birds begin to rouse,   5
And the squirrel from the boughs
Leaps, to get him nuts and fruit ;
The early lark, that erst was mute,
Carols to the rising day
Many a note and many a lay.   10

Unfolding the Flocks

Shepherds, rise, and shake off sleep—
See the blushing morn doth peep
Through the windows, while the sun
To the mountain-tops is run,
Gilding all the vales below   15
With his rising flames, which grow
Greater by his climbing still.—
Up ! ye lazy swains ! and fill
Bag and bottle for the field ;
Clasp your cloaks fast, lest they yield   20
To the bitter north-east wind.
Call the maidens up, and find
Who lies longest, that she may
Be chidden for untimed delay.
Feed your faithful dogs, and pray   25
Heaven to keep you from decay ;
So unfold, and then away.

Folding the Flocks

Shepherds all, and maidens fair,
Fold your flocks up ; for the air
'Gins to thicken, and the sun   30
Already his great course hath run.

3 *subtle*, piercing   8 *erst*, before   10 *lay*, song   26 *decay*, harm

See the dew-drops how they kiss
Every little flower that is ;
Hanging on their velvet heads,
Like a rope of crystal beads.   35
See the heavy clouds low falling,
And bright Hesperus down calling
The dead Night from underground ;
At whose rising, mists unsound,
Damps and vapours, fly apace,   40
Hovering o'er the wanton face
Of these pastures, where they come
Striking dead both bud and bloom :
Therefore from such danger lock
Every one his lovéd flock ;   45
And let your dogs lie loose without,
Lest the wolf come as a scout
From the mountain, and ere day
Bear a lamb or kid away ;
Or the crafty, thievish fox   50
Break upon your simple flocks.
To secure yourself from these
Be not too secure in ease ;
So shall you good shepherds prove,
And deserve your master's love.   55
Now, good night ! may sweetest slumbers
And soft silence fall in numbers
On your eye-lids ! so farewell ;
—Thus I end my evening's knell.

                                   J. Fletcher

* 28 *

THE COUNTRY LIFE

SWEET country life, to such unknown
Whose lives are others', not their own,
But, serving courts and cities, be
Less happy, less enjoying thee :—

7 *Hesperus*, the evening star   39 *unsound*, unhealthy   47 *scout,*

—Thou never plough'st the ocean's foam   5
To seek and bring rough pepper home ;
Nor to the Eastern Ind dost rove
To bring from thence the scorchéd clove ;
Nor, with the loss of thy loved rest,
Bring'st home the ingot from the west :   10
No ! thy ambition's masterpiece
Flies no thought higher than a fleece ;
Or how to pay thy hinds, and clear
All scores, and so to end the year :
But walk'st about thine own dear bounds,   15
Not envying others' larger grounds ;
For well thou know'st 'tis not the extent
Of land makes life, but sweet content.
When now the cock, the ploughman's horn,
Calls forth the lily-wristed morn,   20
Then to thy cornfields thou dost go,
Which though well soil'd, yet thou dost know
That the best compost for the lands
Is the wise master's feet and hands :
There at the plough thou find'st thy team,   25
With a hind whistling there to them ;
And cheer'st them up, by singing how
The kingdom's portion is the plough :
This done, then to th' enamell'd meads
Thou go'st, and as thy foot there treads,   30
Thou seest a present God-like power
Imprinted in each herb and flower ;
And smell'st the breath of great-eyed kine
Sweet as the blossoms of the vine :
Here thou behold'st thy large sleek neat   35
Unto the dew-laps up in meat ;
And as thou look'st, the wanton steer,
The heifer, cow, and ox draw near,
To make a pleasing pastime there :—

---

10 *ingot*, gold or silver bars   11 thy highest wish   17 *extent*, size
20 *lily*, white   23 *compost*, manure   29 *enamell'd*, brightly-coloured

These seen, thou go'st to view thy flocks   40
Of sheep, safe from the wolf and fox,
And find'st their bellies there as full
Of short sweet grass, as backs with wool ;
And leav'st them, as they feed and fill,
A shepherd piping on a hill.   45
For sports, for pageantry and plays,
Thou hast thy eves and holydays ;
On which the young men and maids meet
To exercise their dancing feet,
Tripping the comely country round,   50
With daffodils and daisies crown'd.
Thy wakes, thy quintels, here thou hast,
Thy May-poles too with garlands graced,
Thy morris-dance, thy Whitsun-ale,
Thy shearing-feast, which never fail,   55
Thy harvest home, thy wassail bowl,
That's toss'd up after Fox'i'th'hole,
Thy mummeries, thy twelfth-tide kings
And queens, thy Christmas revellings,—
Thy nut-brown mirth, thy russet wit,   60
And no man pays too dear for it :—
To these, thou hast thy times to go
And trace the hare i'th'treacherous snow ;
Thy witty wiles to draw, and get
The lark into the trammel net ;   65
Thou hast thy cockrood and thy glade
To take the precious pheasant made ;
Thy lime-twigs, snares, and pitfalls then
To catch the pilfering birds, not men.

O happy life ! if that their good   70
The husbandmen but understood ;

46 *pageantry*, shows   52 *quintels*, a game in which poles were run
at a post 54 *morris*, mumming   56 *wassail-bowl*, cup of old ale
57 *Fox*, a game in which boys hopped and flogged each other
60 *russet*, homely   62 Besides   64 *witty*, clever   65 *trammel*,
fowling 66 *cockrood*, see end

Who all the day themselves do please
And younglings, with such sports as these ;
And, lying down, have nought t'affright
Sweet sleep, that makes more short the night. 75

R. Herrick

* 29 *

THE PASSIONATE SHEPHERD TO HIS LOVE

COME live with me and be my Love,
And we will all the pleasures prove
That hills and valleys, dale and field,
And all the craggy mountains yield.

There will we sit upon the rocks   5
And see the shepherds feed their flocks,
By shallow rivers, to whose falls
Melodious birds sing madrigals.

There will I make thee beds of roses
And a thousand fragrant posies,   10
A cap of flowers, and a kirtle
Embroider'd all with leaves of myrtle.

A gown made of the finest wool,
Which from our pretty lambs we pull,
Fair linéd slippers for the cold,   15
With buckles of the purest gold.

A belt of straw and ivy buds
With coral clasps and amber studs :
And if these pleasures may thee move,
Come live with me and be my Love.   20

Thy silver dishes for thy meat
As precious as the gods do eat,
Shall on an ivory table be
Prepared each day for thee and me.

2 *8 madrigals*, short songs   11 *kirtle*, jacket

The shepherd swains shall dance and sing   25
For thy delight each May-morning :
If these delights thy mind may move,
Then live with me and be my Love.

C. Marlowe

* 30 *

THE REAPER

BEHOLD her, single in the field,
Yon solitary Highland Lass !
Reaping and singing by herself ;
Stop here, or gently pass !
Alone she cuts and binds the grain,   5
And sings a melancholy strain ;
O listen ! for the vale profound
Is overflowing with the sound.

No nightingale did ever chaunt
More welcome notes to weary bands   10
Of travellers, in some shady haunt
Among Arabian sands :
No sweeter voice was ever heard
In spring-time from the cuckoo-bird,
Breaking the silence of the seas   15
Among the farthest Hebrides.

Will no one tell me what she sings ?
Perhaps the plaintive numbers flow
For old, unhappy, far-off things,
And battles long ago :   20
Or is it some more humble lay,   -
Familiar matter of to-day ?
Some natural sorrow, loss, or pain,
That has been, and may be again ?

Whate'er the theme, the maiden sang   25
As if her song could have no ending ;
I saw her singing at her work,
And o'er the sickle bending ;

25 *theme*, subject of her song

I listen'd till I had my fill ;
And as I mounted up the hill   30
The music in my heart I bore
Long after it was heard no more.

W. Wordsworth

* 31 *

NEW AND OLD

GLAD sight, wherever new with old
Is join'd through some dear homeborn tie ;
The life of all that we behold
Depends upon that mystery.
Vain is the glory of the sky,   5
The beauty vain of field and grove,
Unless, while with admiring eye
We gaze, we also learn to love.

W. Wordsworth

* 32 *

AUTUMN

A Dirge

The warm sun is failing, the bleak wind is wailing,
The bare boughs are sighing, the pale flowers are
    dying ;
              And the year
On the earth her death-bed, in a shroud of leaves
    dead,
              Is lying.   5
        Come, Months, come away,
        From November to May.
        In your saddest array,—
        Follow the bier
        Of the dead cold year,   10
And like dim shadows watch by her sepulchre.

8 *array*, dress   11 *sepulchre*, tomb

The chill rain is falling, the nipt worm is crawling,
The rivers are swelling, the thunder is knelling,
   For the year;
The blithe swallows are flown, and the lizards each
 gone   15
    To his dwelling.
   Come, Months, come away;
   Put on white, black, and gray;
   Let your light sisters play;
   Ye, follow the bier   20
   Of the dead cold year,
And make her grave green with tear on tear.
        P. B. Shelley

* 33 *

THE COUNTRYMAN

WHAT pleasures have great princes
 More dainty to their choice,
Than herdmen wild, who careless
 In quiet life rejoice;
And fortune's favours scorning,   5
Sing sweet in summer morning.

All day their flocks each tendeth;
 At night they take their rest;
More quiet than who sendeth
 His ship into the east,   10
Where gold and pearl are plenty,
But getting very dainty.

For lawyers and their pleading,
 They 'steem it not a straw :—
They think that honest meaning   15
 Is of itself a law :
Where conscience judgeth plainly,
They spend no money vainly.

   19 the summer months
 12 *dainty*, difficult   14 *'steem*, value

O happy who thus liveth,
  Not caring much for gold ;   20
With clothing, which sufficeth
  To keep him from the cold :—
Though poor and plain his diet,
Yet merry it is and quiet.

                        Unknown

* 34 *

TO A MOUNTAIN DAISY

WEE, modest, crimson-tippéd flower,
Thou's met me in an evil hour ;
For I maun crush amang the stour
      Thy slender stem ;
To spare thee now is past my power,   5
      Thou bonnie gem.

Alas ! it's no thy neebor sweet,
The bonnie lark, companion meet !
Bending thee 'mang the dewy weet
      Wi' spreckled breast,   10
When upward springing, blythe, to greet
      The purpling east.

Cauld blew the bitter-biting north
Upon thy early, humble, birth ;
Yet cheerfully thou glinted forth   15
      Amid the storm ;
Scarce rear'd above the parent earth
      Thy tender form.

The flaunting flowers our gardens yield
High sheltering woods and wa's maun shield, 20
But thou beneath the random bield
      O' clod or stane
Adorns the histie stibble-field,
      Unseen, alane.

3 *maun*, must : *stour*, dust   7 *no*, not : *neebor*, neighbour
8 *meet*, fit   9 *weet*, wet   10 *spreckled*, speckled
12 *purpling*, at dawn   15 *glinted*, glanced
20 *wa's*, walls 21 *bield*, shelter 23 *histie*, dry : *stibble*, stubble

There, in thy scanty mantle clad,   25
Thy snawy bosom sunward spread,
Thou lifts thy unassuming head
         In humble guise ;
But now the share uptears thy bed,
         And low thou lies !   30

R. Burns

* 35 *

THE WHIRL-BLAST

A WHIRL-BLAST from behind the hill
Rush'd o'er the wood with startling sound ;
Then—all at once the air was still,
And showers of hailstones patter'd round.
Where leafless oaks tower'd high above,   5
I sat within an undergrove
Of tallest hollies, tall and green ;
A fairer bower was never seen.
From year to year the spacious floor
With wither'd leaves is cover'd o'er,   10
And all the year the bower is green ;
But see ! where'er the hailstones drop
The wither'd leaves all skip and hop ;
There's not a breeze—no breath of air—
Yet here, and there, and every where   15
Along the floor, beneath the shade
By those embowering hollies made,
The leaves in myriads jump and spring,
As if with pipes and music rare
Some Robin Goodfellow were there,   20
And all those leaves, in festive glee,
Were dancing to the minstrelsy.

W. Wordsworth

27 *unassuming*, modest   28 *guise*, manner
20 *Robin Goodfellow*, a fairy   22 *minstrelsy*, music

* 36

WINTER

WHEN icicles hang by the wall,
  And Dick the shepherd blows his nail,
And Tom bears logs into the hall,
  And milk comes frozen home in pail ;
When blood is nipt, and ways be foul,   5
Then nightly sings the staring owl
      Tuwhoo !
Tuwhit ! tuwhoo !   A merry note !
While greasy Joan doth keel the pot.

When all around the wind doth blow,   10
  And coughing drowns the parson's saw,
And birds sit brooding in the snow,
  And Marian's nose looks red and raw ;
When roasted crabs hiss in the bowl—
Then nightly sings the staring owl .   15
      Tuwhoo !
Tuwhit ! tuwhoo !   A merry note !
While greasy Joan doth keel the pot.

                      W. Shakespeare

* 37 *

JOCK OF HAZELDEAN

' WHY weep ye by the tide, ladie ?
  ' Why weep ye by the tide ?
' I'll wed ye to my youngest son,
  ' And ye sall be his bride :
' And ye sall be his bride, ladie,   5
  ' Sae comely to be seen '—
But aye she loot the tears down fa'
  For Jock of Hazeldean.

9 *keel*, skim   11 *saw*, speech   14 *crabs*, wild apples
        7 *loot*, let : *fa'* fall

'Now let this wilfu' grief be done,
  'And dry that cheek so pale ;   10
'Young Frank is chief of Errington,
  'And lord of Langley-dale ;
'His step is first in peaceful ha',
  'His sword in battle keen '—
But aye she loot the tears down fa'   15
  For Jock of Hazeldean.

'A chain of gold ye sall not lack,
  'Nor braid to bind your hair,
'Nor mettled hound, nor managed hawk,
  'Nor palfrey fresh and fair ;   20
'And you the foremost o' them a'
  'Sall ride our forest-queen '—
But aye she loot the tears down fa'
  For Jock of Hazeldean.

The kirk was deck'd at morning-tide,   25
  The tapers glimmer'd fair ;
The priest and bridegroom wait the bride,
  And dame and knight are there :
They sought her baith by bower and ha' ;
  The ladie was not seen !   30
She's o'er the Border, and awa'
  Wi' Jock of Hazeldean.

                              Sir W. Scott

* 38 *

THE OUTLAW

O BRIGNALL banks are wild and fair,
  And Greta woods are green,
And you may gather garlands there
  Would grace a summer-queen.

13 *ha'*, hall, for house   19 *mettled*, spirited : *managed*, trained
25 *kirk*, church   29 *bower*, lady's own rown
    Outlaw, man driven out to live by himself, a robber

And as I rode by Dalton-Hall   5
  Beneath the turrets high,
A Maiden on the castle-wall
  Was singing merrily :
' O Brignall Banks are fresh and fair,
  ' And Greta woods are green ;   10
' I'd rather rove with Edmund there
  ' Than reign our English queen.'

—' If, Maiden, thou wouldst wend with me,
  ' To leave both tower and town,
' Thou first must guess what life lead we   15
  ' That dwell by dale and down.
' And if thou canst that riddle read,
  ' As read full well you may,
' Then to the greenwood shalt thou speed
  ' As blithe as Queen of May.'   20
Yet sung she, ' Brignall banks are fair,
  ' And Greta woods are green ;
' I'd rather rove with Edmund there
  ' Than reign our English queen.'

' I read you by your bugle-horn   25
  ' And by your palfrey good,
' I read you for a ranger sworn
  ' To keep the king's greenwood.'
—' A Ranger, lady, winds his horn,
  ' And 'tis at peep of light ;   30
' His blast is heard at merry morn,
  ' And mine at dead of night.'
Yet sung she ' Brignall banks are fair,
  ' And Greta woods are gay ;
' I would I were with Edmund there   35
  ' To reign his Queen of May !

---

13 *wend*, go   25 *read*, declare   26 *palfrey*, pony
27 *ranger*, forest-keeper   28 *keep*, guard   29 *winds*, blows

' With burnish'd brand and musketoon
  ' So gallantly you come.
' I read you for a bold Dragoon
  ' That lists the tuck of drum.'   40
—' I list no more the tuck of drum,
  ' No more the trumpet hear ;
' But when the beetle sounds his hum
  ' My comrades take the spear.
' And O ! though Brignall banks be fair   45
  ' And Greta woods be gay,
' Yet mickle must the maiden dare
  ' Would reign my Queen of May !

' Maiden ! a nameless life I lead,
  ' A nameless death I'll die !   50
' The fiend whose lantern lights the mead
  ' Were better mate than I !
' And when I'm with my comrades met
  ' Beneath the greenwood bough
' What once we were we all forget,   55
  ' Nor think what we are now.'

Chorus

Yet Brignall banks are fresh and fair,
  And Greta woods are green,
And you may gather garlands there
  Would grace a summer-queen.   60
                              Sir W. Scott

* 39 *

EDWIN AND ANGELINA

' TURN, gentle Hermit of the dale,
  ' And guide my lonely way
' To where yon taper cheers the vale
  ' With hospitable ray.

37 *brand*, sword : *musketoon*, blunderbuss   40 *tuck*, beat

'For here forlorn and lost I tread,   5
  'With fainting steps and slow,
'Where wilds, immeasurably spread,
  'Seem lengthening as I go.'

—'Forbear, my son,' the Hermit cries,
  'To tempt the dangerous gloom,   10
'For yonder faithless phantom flies
  'To lure thee to thy doom.

Here to the houseless child of want
  'My door is open still ;
'And though my portion is but scant   15
  'I give it with goodwill.

'Then turn to-night, and freely share
  'Whate'er my cell bestows ;
'My rushy couch and frugal fare,
  'My blessing and repose.   20

'No flocks that range the valley free
  'To slaughter I condemn ;
'Taught by that Power that pities me,
  'I learn to pity them :

'But from the mountain's grassy side   25
  'A guiltless feast I bring :
'A scrip with herbs and fruits supplied,
  'And water from the spring.

'Then, pilgrim ! turn ; thy cares forego;
  'All earth-born cares are wrong: 30
'Man wants but little here below,
  'Nor wants that little long.'

7 *immeasurably*, without end   10 *tempt*, try
11 the Will-o'-the-Wisp   12 *lure*, tempt
19 bed of rushes   22 kill
27 *scrip*, little bag   29 *forego*, lay by

Soft as the dew from heaven descends
    His gentle accents fell :
The modest stranger lowly bends,   35
    And follows to the cell.

Far in a wilderness-obscure
    The lonely mansion lay,
A refuge to the neighbouring poor,
    And strangers led astray.   40

No stores beneath its humble thatch
    Required a master's care,
The wicket, opening with a latch,
    Received the harmless pair.

And now, when busy crowds retire   45
    To take their evening rest,
The hermit trimm'd his little fire,
    And cheer'd his pensive guest:

And spread his vegetable store,
    And gaily press'd and smiled ;   50
And skill'd in legendary lore,
    The lingering hours beguiled.

Around, in sympathetic mirth,
    Its tricks the kitten tries ;
The cricket chirrups on the hearth,   55
    The crackling fagot flies.

But nothing could a charm impart
    To soothe the stranger's woe ;
For grief was heavy at his heart,
    And tears began to flow.   60

His rising cares the Hermit spied,
    With answering care oppress'd :
And 'Whence, unhappy youth,' he cried,
    'The sorrows of thy breast?

34 *accents*, voice   48 *pensive*, thoughtful
51 *legendary lore*, ancient stories   53 cheerful like the Hermit
57 *impart*, give   62 similar sadness

'From better habitations spurn'd   65
  'Reluctant dost thou rove?
'Or grieve for friendship unreturn'd,
  'Or unregarded love?

'Alas! the joys that fortune brings
  'Are trifling, and decay;   70
'And those who prize the paltry things,
  'More trifling still than they.

'And what is friendship but a name,
  'A charm that lulls to sleep;
'A shade that follows wealth or fame,   75
  'But leaves the wretch to weep?

'And love is still an emptier sound,
  'The modern fair-one's jest;
'On earth unseen, or only found
  'To warm the turtle's nest.   80

'For shame, fond youth! thy sorrows hush;
  'And spurn the sex,' he said;
But while he spoke, a rising blush
  His love-lorn guest betray'd!

Surprised he sees new beauties rise,   85
  Swift mantling to the view;
Like colours o'er the morning skies,
  As bright, as transient too.

The bashful look, the rising breast,
  Alternate spread alarms: 90
The lovely stranger stands confess'd,
  A maid in all her charms.

And 'Ah! forgive a stranger rude,—
  'A wretch forlorn,' she cried;
'Whose feet, unhallow'd, thus intrude   95
  'Where Heaven and you reside!

65 *spurn'd*, driven   66 *reluctant*, unwilling   69 *fortune*,wealth
82 *the sex*, women   86 *mantling*, spreading
88 *transient*, soon passing   91 *confess'd*, revealed   95 *intrude*, push in

' But let a maid thy pity share,
  Whom love has taught to stray;
' Who seeks for rest, but finds despair
  ' Companion of her way.   100

' My father lived beside the Tyne,
  ' A wealthy lord was he ;
' And all his wealth was mark'd as mine,
  ' He had but only me.

' To win me from his tender arms   105
  ' Unnumber'd suitors came,
' Who praised me for imputed charms,
  ' And felt or feign'd a flame.

' Each hour a mercenary crowd
  ' With richest proffers strove :   110
' Amongst the rest, young Edwin bow'd,
  ' But never talk'd of love.

' In humble, simple habit clad,
  ' No wealth nor power had he :
' Wisdom and worth were all he had,   115
  ' But these were all to me.

' And when, beside me in the dale,
  ' He caroll'd lays of love,
' His breath lent fragrance to the gale,
  ' And music to the grove.   120

' The blossom opening to the day,
  ' The dews of heaven refined,
' Could nought of purity display
  ' To emulate his mind.

' The dew, the blossom on the tree,   125
  ' With charms inconstant shine :
' Their charms were his ; but, woe to me !
  ' Their constancy was mine.

107 *imputed*, which they said they saw   108 *flame*, love
109 *mercenary*, greedy of money   110 *proffers*, offers
124 *emulate*, rival   126 changeable beauties

'For still I tried each fickle art,
  'Importunate and vain ;   130
'And, while his passion touch'd my heart,
  'I triumph'd in his pain :

'Till, quite dejected with my scorn,
  'He left me to my pride ;
'And sought a solitude forlorn,   135
  'In secret, where he died.

'But mine the sorrow, mine the fault !
  'And well my life shall pay;
'I'll seek the solitude he sought,
  'And stretch me where he lay.   140

'And there, forlorn, despairing, hid,
  'I'll lay me down and die ;
''Twas so for me that Edwin did,
  'And so for him will I.'

—'Forbid it, Heaven !' the Hermit cried, 145
  And clasp'd her to his breast :
The wondering fair one turn'd to chide—
  'Twas Edwin's self that press'd !

'Turn, Angelina, ever dear,
  'My charmer, turn to see   150
'Thy own, thy long-lost Edwin here,
  'Restored to love and thee.

'Thus let me hold thee to my heart,
  'And every care resign :
'And shall we never, never part,   155
  'My life—my all that's mine ?

'No, never from this hour to part,
  'We'll live and love so true :
'The sigh that rends thy constant heart
  'Shall break thy Edwin's too.'   160

                                 O. Goldsmith

132 *triumph'd*, rejoiced   133 *dejected*, grieved

* 40 *

THE LASS OF LOCHROYAN

· O WHO will shoe my bonny foot,
 'And who will glove my hand ?
And who will lace my middle jimp.
 'Wi' a long, long, linen band ?

'Or who will kaim my yellow hair   5
 'Wi' a new-made silver kaim ?
'O who will father my young son
 'Till Lord Gregory comes hame ?

'O if I had a bonny ship,
 'And men to sail wi' me,   10
'It's I would gang to my true Love,
 'Since he winna come to me !'

Then she's gar'd build a bonny boat,
 To sail the salt, salt sea :
The sails were of the light-green silk,   15
 And the ropes of taffetie.

She had not been on the sea sailing
 About a month or more,
Till landed has she her bonny ship
 Near to her true Love's door.   20

She's ta'en her young son in her arms
 And to the door she's gane ;
And long she knock'd, and sair she call'd,
 But answer got she nane.

'O open the door, Lord Gregory !   25
 'O open, and let me in !
'For the wind blows through my yellow hair,
 'And the rain drops o'er my chin.'

3 *middle jimp*, slender waist   5 *kaim*, comb   12 *winna*, will not
12 *gar'd*, made   16 *taffetie*, thin silk   23 *sair*, sorely

Long stood she at Lord Gregory's door,
   And long she tirl'd the pin ;   30
At length up gat his false mother,
   Says, ' Who's that would be in ?'

—' O it's Annie of Lochroyan,
   ' Your Love, come o'er the sea,
' But and your young son in her arms ;   35
   ' So open the door to me.'

—' Away, away, ye ill woman !
   ' You're not come here for gude ;
' You're but a witch, or a vile warlock,
   ' Or a mermaid o' the flood.'   40

—' I'm no a witch, nor vile warlock,
   ' Nor mermaiden,' said she ;
' But I am Annie of Lochroyan,—
   ' O open the door to me !'

—' If thou be Annie of Lochroyan   45
   ' (As I trow ye binna she),
' Now tell me some of the love-tokens
   ' That pass'd 'tween me and thee.'

—' O dinna ye mind, Lord Gregory,
   ' As we sat at the wine,   50
' How we changed the rings from our fingers,
   ' And I can show thee thine ?

' O yours was good, and good enough,
   ' But not so good as mine ;
' For yours was o' the good red gold,   55
   ' But mine of the diamond fine.

' So open the door, Love Gregory,
   ' And open it with speed ;
' Or your young son that's in my arms,
   ' For cold will soon be dead.'   60

30 *tirl'd*, twisted the latch
35 *But and*, and also   39 *warlock*, wizard
46 *binna*, be not   49 *dinna*, do not

—' Away, away, ye ill woman !
' Go from my door for shame !
' For I have gotten another Love,
' So you may hie you hame.'

Fair Annie turn'd her round about ;   65
' Well ! since that it be sae,
' May never a woman, that has borne a son,
' Have a heart so full of wae !

' Take down, take down, the mast of gold,
' Set up the mast o' tree ;   70
' It ill becomes a forsaken lady
' To sail so gallantlie.'

Lord Gregory started from his sleep,
And to his mother did say,
' I dreamt a dream, this night, mother,   75
' That makes my heart right wae.

' I dreamt that Annie of Lochroyan,
' The flower of all her kin,
' E'en now was standing at my door,
' But none would let her in.'   80

—' O there was a woman stood at the door,
' With a bairn intill her arm ;
' But I could not let her come within,
' For fear she had done you harm.'

—' O wae betide ye, ill woman !   85
' An ill death may ye dee !
' That wadna open the door to her,
Nor yet would waken me !'

O, he's gone down to yon shore side
As fast as he could fare ;   90
He saw fair Annie in the boat,
But the wind it toss'd her sair.

63 *wae*, woe   70 *tree*, wood   76 *wae*, sad

And ' hey, Annie !' and ' how, Annie !'
  ' O Annie, winna ye bide ?'
But aye the mair he cried 'Annie,'   95
  The broader grew the tide.

And ' hey, Annie !' and ' how, Annie !'
  ' O Annie, speak to me !'
But aye the louder he cried 'Annie,'
  The louder roar'd the sea.   100

The wind blew loud, the sea grew rough,
  And the ship was rent in twain :
And soon he saw his fair Annie
  Come floating o'er the main.

He saw his young son in her arms,   105
  Both toss'd above the tide ;
He wrang his hands, and fast he ran
  And plunged in the sea sae wide.

He catch'd her by the yellow hair,
  And drew her up on the sand ;   110
But cold and stiff was every limb
  Before he reach'd the land.

And then he kiss'd her on the cheek,
  And kiss'd her on the chin ;
And sair he kiss'd her on the lips ;   115
  But there was no breath within.

' O wae betide my cruel mother !
  ' An ill death may she dee !
' She turn'd fair Annie from my door,
  ' Wha died for love of me !'   120

               Unknown

94 *bide*, wait

* 41 *

CUMNOR HALL

THE dews of summer night did fall ;
   The moon, sweet Regent of the sky,
Silver'd the walls of Cumnor Hall,
   And many an oak that grew thereby.

Now nought was heard beneath the skies ;   5
   The sounds of busy life were still,
Save an unhappy lady's sighs
   That issued from that lonely pile.

' Leicester ! ' she cried, ' is this thy love
   ' That thou so oft hast sworn to me,   10
' To leave me in this lonely grove,
   ' Immured in shameful privity ?

' No more thou com'st with lover's speed
   ' Thy once-belovéd bride to see ;
' But, be she alive, or be she dead,   15
   ' I fear, stern Earl, 's the same to thee.

' Not so the usage I received
   ' When happy in my father's hall :
' No faithless husband then me grieved ;
   ' No chilling fears did me appal.   20

' I rose up with the cheerful morn,
   ' No lark more blithe, no flower more gay :
' And like the bird that haunts the thorn,
   ' So merrily sung the live-long day.

' If that my beauty is but small,   25
   ' Among court-ladies all despised ;
' Why didst thou rend it from that hall
   ' Where, scornful Earl ! it well was prized ?

2 *regent*, ruler   8 *issued*, came forth : *pile*, building
12 *immured*, buried : *privity*, solitude
17 *usage*, treatment   20 *appal*, frighten   27 *rend*, take away

' But, Leicester, (or I much am wrong),
    ' Or 'tis not beauty lures thy vows ;   30
' Rather, ambition's gilded crown
    ' Makes thee forget thy humble spouse.

' Then, Leicester, why,—again I plead,
    ' The injured surely may repine,—
' Why didst thou wed a country maid,   35
    ' When some fair Princess might be thine ?

' Why didst thou praise my humble charms,
    ' And O ! then leave them to decay?
' Why didst thou win me to thy arms,
    ' Then leave to mourn the live-long day ?   40

' The village maidens of the plain
    ' Salute me lowly as they go :
' Envious they mark my silken train,
    ' Nor think a Countess can have woe.

' How far less blest am I than them !   45
    ' Daily to pine and waste with care,
' Like the poor plant, that, from its stem
    ' Divided, feels the chilling air.

' My spirits flag ; my hopes decay ;
    ' Still that dread death-bell smites my ear : 50
' And many a boding seems to say
    ' Countess, prepare ! thy end is near ! '

Thus sore and sad the Lady grieved
    In Cumnor Hall so lone and drear ;
And many a heartfelt sigh she heaved,   55
    And let fall many a bitter tear.

And ere the dawn of day appear'd,
    In Cumnor Hall so lone and drear,
Full many a piercing scream was heard,
    And many a cry of mortal fear.   60

30 *lures*, tempts thy wishes   32 *spouse*, wife
34 *repine*, murmur   37 *charms*, beauties   42 bow to me
43 *train*, dress   49 *flag*, sink   51 *boding*, sign

The death-bell thrice was heard to ring ;
  An aerial voice was heard to call ;
And thrice the raven flapp'd its wing
  Around the towers of Cumnor Hall.

The mastiff howl'd at village door ;   65
  The oaks were shatter'd on the green ;
Woe was the hour ! for never more
  That hapless Countess e'er was seen.

And in that manor now no more
  Is cheerful feast and sprightly ball :   70
For ever since that dreary hour
  Have spirits haunted Cumnor Hall.

The village maids, with fearful glance,
  Avoid the ancient moss-grown wall,
Nor ever lead the merry dance   75
  Among the groves of Cumnor Hall.

Full many a traveller oft hath sigh'd,
  And pensive wept the Countess' fall,
As wandering onwards they've espied
  The haunted towers of Cumnor Hall.   80
                      W. J. Mickle

* 42 *

THE TRUE AND THE FALSE

WHERE shall the lover rest
  Whom the fates sever
From his true maiden's breast
  Parted for ever ?
Where, through groves deep and high   5
  Sounds the far billow,
Where early violets die
  Under the willow :—
    Eleu loro
  Soft shall be his pillow.   10

There, through the summer day
  Cool streams are laving :
There, while the tempests sway,
  Scarce are boughs waving ;
There thy rest shalt thou take,   15
  Parted for ever,
Never again to wake
  Never, O never !
    Eleu loro
  Never, O never !   20

—Where shall the traitor rest,
  He, the deceiver,
Who could win maiden's breast,
  Ruin, and leave her ?
In the lost battle,   25
  Borne down by the flying,
Where mingles war's rattle
  With groans of the dying ;
    Eleu loro
  There shall he be lying.   30

Her wing shall the eagle flap
  O'er the falsehearted ;
His warm blood the wolf shall lap
  Ere life be parted :
Shame and dishonour sit   35
  By his grave ever ;
Blessing shall hallow it
  Never, O never !
    Eleu loro
  Never, O never !   40

                     Sir W. Scott

* 43 *

AULD ROBIN GRAY

WHEN the sheep are in the fauld, and the kye at
    hame,
And a' the warld to rest are gane,
The waes o' my heart fa' in showers frae my e'e,
While my gudeman lies sound by me.

Young Jamie lo'ed me weel, and sought me for his
    bride ;   5
But saving a croun he had naething else beside :
To make the croun a pund, young Jamie gaed to
    sea ;
And the croun and the pund were baith for me.

He hadna been awa' a week but only twa,
When my father brak his arm, and the cow was
    stown awa' ;   10
My mother she fell sick, and my Jamie at the sea —
And auld Robin Gray came a-courtin' me.

My father couldna work, and my mother couldna
    spin ;
I toil'd day and night, but their bread I couldna
    win ;
Auld Rob maintain'd them baith, and wi' tears in
    his e'e   15
' Said, Jennie, for their sakes, O, marry me ! '

My heart it said nay ; I look'd for Jamie back ;
But the wind it blew high, and the ship it was a
    wrack ;
His ship it was a wrack—why didna Jamie dee ?
Or why do I live to cry, Wae's me ?   20

1 *fauld*, fold : *kye*, cattle	3 *fa'*, fall	7 *gaed*, went
9 *awa'*, away a fortnight		10 *stown*, stolen
13 *couldna*, could not		19 *dee*, die

My father urgit sair : my mother didna speak ;
But she look'd in my face till my heart was like to
    break :
They gi'ed him my hand, but my heart was at the
    sea :
Sae auld Robin Gray he was gudeman to me.

I hadna been a wife a week but only four,   25
When mournfu' as I sat on the stane at the door,
I saw my Jamie's wraith, for I couldna think it he—
Till he said, ' I'm come hame to marry thee.'

—O sair, sair did we greet, and muckle did we say ;
We took but ae kiss, and I bad him gang away : 30
I wish that I were dead, but I'm no like to dee ;
And why was I born to say, Wae's me !

I gang like a ghaist, and I carena to spin ;
I daurna think on Jamie, for that wad be a sin ;
But I'll do my best a gude wife aye to be,   35
For auld Robin Gray he is kind unto me.
                       Lady A. Lindsay

* 44 *

WILLY DROWNED IN YARROW

Down in yon garden sweet and gay
    Where bonnie grows the lily,
I heard a fair maid sighing say,
    ' My wish be wi' sweet Willie !

' Willie's rare, and Willie's fair,   5
    ' And Willie's wondrous bonny ;
' And Willie hecht to marry me
    ' Gin e'er he married ony.

---

21 *urgit*, pressed   24 *gudeman*, husband   27 *wraith*, ghost
29 *sair*, sorely : *greet*, cry : *muckle*, much   31 *like*, likely
34 *daurna*, dare not   7 *hecht*, promised   8 *gin*, if : *ony*, any

' O gentle wind, that bloweth south,
  ' From where my Love repaireth,   10
' Convey a kiss frae his dear mouth
  ' And tell me how he fareth !

' O tell sweet Willie to come doun
  ' And hear the mavis singing,
' And see the birds on ilka bush   15
  ' And leaves around them hinging.

' The lav'rock there, wi' her white breast
  ' And gentle throat sae narrow :
' There's sport eneuch for gentlemen
  ' On Leader-haughs and Yarrow.   20

' O Leader-haughs are wide and braid
  ' And Yarrow-haughs are bonny ;
' There Willie hecht to marry me
  ' If e'er he married ony.

' But Willie's gone, whom I thought on,   25
  ' And does not hear me weeping ;
' Draws many a tear frae true love's e'e
  ' When other maids are sleeping.

' O came ye by yon water-side ?
  ' Pou'd you the rose or lily ?   30
' Or came you by yon meadow green,
  ' Or saw you my sweet Willie ?'

She sought him up, she sought him down,
  She sought him braid and narrow ;
Syne, in the cleaving of a craig,   35
  She found him drown'd in Yarrow !

                   Unknown

---

10 *repaireth*, is going   14 *mavis*, thrush   15 *ilka*, every
17 *lav'rock*, lark   19 *eneuch*, enough   20 *haughs*, water-meadows
21 *braid*, broad   30 *pou'd*, pulled
34 through plain and valley   35 *syne*, then : *craig*, rock

* 45 *

LORD ULLIN'S DAUGHTER

A CHIEFTAIN to the Highlands bound
Cries ' Boatman, do not tarry !
' And I'll give thee a silver pound
' To row us o'er the ferry ! '

—' Now, who be ye, would cross Lochgyle   5
' This dark and stormy water ? '
—' O I'm the chief of Ulva's isle,
' And this, Lord Ullin's daughter.

' And fast before her father's men
' Three days we've fled together,   10
' For should he find us in the glen,
' My blood would stain the heather.

' His horsemen hard behind us ride—
' Should they our steps discover,
' Then who will cheer my bonny bride   15
' When they have slain her lover ? '

Out spoke the hardy Highland wight,
' I'll go, my chief, I'm ready:
' It is not for your silver bright,
' But for your winsome lady:—   20

' And by my word ! the bonny bird
' In danger shall not tarry ;
' So though the waves are raging white,
' I'll row you o'er the ferry.'

By this the storm grew loud apace,   25
The water-wraith was shrieking ;
And in the scowl of heaven each face
Grew dark as they were speaking.

26 *water-wraith.* spirit of the lake   27 *scowl,* storminess

But still as wilder blew the wind,
And as the night grew drearer,   30
Adown the glen rode arméd men,
Their trampling sounded nearer.

' O haste thee, haste !' the lady cries,
' Though tempests round us gather ;
' I'll meet the raging of the skies,   35
' But not an angry father !'

The boat has left a stormy land,
A stormy sea before her,—
When, O ! too strong for human hand
The tempest gather'd o'er her.   40

And still they row'd amidst the roar
Of waters fast prevailing :
Lord Ullin reach'd that fatal shore,—
His wrath was changed to wailing.

For, sore dismay'd, through storm and shade 45
His child he did discover :—
One lovely hand she stretch'd for aid,
And one was round her lover.

' Come back ! come back !' he cried in grief
' Across this stormy water :   50
' And I'll forgive your Highland chief :—
' My daughter !—O my daughter !'

'Twas vain : the loud waves lash'd the shore,
Return or aid preventing :
The waters wild went o'er his child,   55
And he was left lamenting.

                                    T. Campbell

* 46 *

THE DESTRUCTION OF SENNACHERIB

THE Assyrian came down like the wolf on the fold,
And his cohorts were gleaming in purple and
gold,
And the sheen of their spears was like stars on the
sea,
When the blue wave rolls nightly on deep Galilee.

Like the leaves of the forest when summer is
green,   5
That host with their banners at sunset were seen ;
Like the leaves of the forest when autumn hath
blown,
That host on the morrow lay wither'd and strown.

For the Angel of Death spread his wings on the
blast,
And breathed in the face of the foe as he pass'd; 10
And the eyes of the sleepers wax'd deadly and chill,
And their hearts but once heaved, and for ever grew
still.

And there lay the steed with his nostril all wide,
But through it there roll'd not the breath of his
pride ;
And the foam of his gasping lay white on the
turf,   15
And cold as the spray of the rock-beating surf.

And there lay the rider, distorted and pale,
With the dew on his brow, and the rust on his
mail ;
And the tents were all silent, the banners alone,
The lances unlifted, the trumpet unblown.   20

2 *cohorts*, regiments   3 *sheen*, shining   11 *wax'd*, grew
13 *steed*, warhorse   16 *surf*, waves
17 *distorted*, twisted in death   18 *mail*, armour

And the widows of Ashur are loud in their wail,
And the idols are broke in the temple of Baal,
And the might of the Gentile, unsmote by the
    sword,
Hath melted like snow in the glance of the Lord !
                      Lord Byron

* 47 *

THE SPANISH ARMADA

ATTEND all ye who list to hear our noble England's
    praise,
I tell of the thrice famous deeds she wrought in
    ancient days,
When that great fleet invincible against her bore in
    vain
The richest spoils of Mexico, the stoutest hearts
    of Spain.

It was about the lovely close of a warm summer
    day,   5
There came a gallant merchant-ship full sail to
    Plymouth Bay ;
Her crew hath seen Castile's black fleet beyond
    Aurigny's isle,
At earliest twilight, on the waves lie heaving many
    a mile ;
At sunrise she escaped their van, by God's especial
    grace ;
And the tall Pinta, till the noon, had held her close
    in chase.   10
Forthwith a guard at every gun was placed along
    the wall ;
The beacon blazed upon the roof of Edgecumbe's
    lofty hall ;

21 *Ashur*, Assyria   1 *list*, desire   7 *isle*, Alderney
                    9 *van*, foremost ships

Many a light fishing-bark put out to pry along the
    coast ;

And with loose rein and bloody spur rode inland
    many a post.

With his white hair unbonnet'd the stout old
    sheriff comes ;   15

Behind him march the halberdiers, before him
    sound the drums ;

His yeomen, round the market-cross, make clear
    an ample space,

For there behoves him to set up the standard of
    her Grace.

And haughtily the trumpets peal, and gaily dance
    the bells,

As slow upon the labouring wind the royal blazon
    swells.   20

Look how the Lion of the sea lifts up his ancient
    crown,

And underneath his deadly paw treads the gay
    Lilies down.

So stalk'd he when he turn'd to flight on that
    famed Picard field

Bohemia's plume, and Genoa's bow, and Cæsar's
    eagle shield :

So glared he when at Agincourt in wrath he turn'd
    to bay,   25

And crush'd and torn beneath his claws the princely
    hunters lay.

Ho ! strike the flag-staff deep, Sir Knight ; ho !
    scatter flowers, fair maids :

Ho ! gunners, fire a loud salute : ho ! gallants, draw
    your blades ;

14 *post*, messenger   16 *halberdiers*, guards with axes
17 *yeomen*, stout followers
18 *standard*, great flag : *her Grace*, Queen Elizabeth
20 *blazon*, arms of England   22 *lilies*, old arms of France
23 *field*, Cressy   28 *salute*, volley : *blades*, swords

Thou sun, shine on her joyously—ye breezes waft
    her wide ;
Our glorious SEMPER EADEM—the banner of
    our pride.
The freshening breeze of eve unfurl'd that ban-
    ner's massive fold,
The parting gleam of sunshine kiss'd that haughty
    scroll of gold ;
Night sank upon the dusky beach, and on the
    purple sea,—
Such night in England ne'er had been, nor e'er
    again shall be !
From Eddystone to Berwick bounds, from Lynn to
    Milford Bay,   35
That time of slumber was as bright and busy as
    the day ;
For swift to east and swift to west the ghastly
    war-flame spread ;
High on Saint Michael's Mount it shone—it shone
    on Beachy Head.
Far on the deep the Spaniard saw, along each
    southern shire,
Cape beyond cape, in endless range, those twink-
    ling points of fire ;   40
The fisher left his skiff to rock on Tamar's glittering
    waves,
The rugged miners pour'd to war from Mendip's
    sunless caves.
O'er Longleat's towers, o'er Cranbourne's oaks, the
    fiery herald flew ;
He roused the shepherds of Stonehenge, the rangers
    of Beaulieu.
Right sharp and quick the bells all night rang out
    from Bristol town,   45
And ere the day three hundred horse had met on
    Clifton down ;

The sentinel on Whitehall-gate look'd forth into
    the night,
And saw o'erhanging Richmond Hill, the streak of
    blood-red light.
Then bugle's note and cannon's roar the death-like
    silence broke,
And with one start, and with one cry, the royal city
    woke.   50
At once on all her stately gates arose the answering
    fires ;
At once the wild alarum clash'd from all her reel-
    ing spires ;
From all the batteries of the Tower peal'd loud the
    voice of fear ;
And all the thousand masts of Thames sent back
    a louder cheer :
And from the furthest wards was heard the rush of
    hurrying feet,   55
And the broad streams of pikes and flags rush'd
    down each roaring street :
And broader still became the blaze, and louder
    still the din,
As fast from every village round the horse came
    spurring in :
And eastward straight, from wild Blackheath, the
    warlike errand went,
And roused in many an ancient hall the gallant
    squires of Kent.   60
Southward, from Surrey's pleasant hills flew those
    bright couriers forth ;
High on bleak Hampstead's swarthy moor they
    started for the North ;
And on, and on, without a pause, untired they
    bounded still,

50 *city*, London   52 *reeling*, trembling under the sound
55 *wards*, divisions of the city   56 *pikes*, spears   58 *horse*, soldiers
59 *errand*, the beacon-fires to rouse England : so
61 *couriers*   62 *swarthy*, dark   63 *paus*, *stay*

All night from tower to tower they sprang ; they
    sprang from hill to hill :
Till the proud Peak unfurl'd the flag o'er Darwin's
    rocky dales,   65
Till like volcanoes flared to Heaven the stormy hills
    of Wales ;
Till twelve fair counties saw the blaze on Malvern's
    lonely height,
Till stream'd in crimson on the wind the Wrekin's
    crest of light,
Till broad and fierce the star came forth on Ely's
    stately fane,
And tower and hamlet rose in arms o'er all the
    boundless plain ;   70
Till Belvoir's lordly terraces the sign to Lincoln sent,
And Lincoln sped the message on o'er the wide vale
    of Trent ;
Till Skiddaw saw the fire that burn'd on Gaunt's
    embattled pile,
And the red glare on Skiddaw roused the burghers
    of Carlisle.

Lord Macaulay

* 48 *

HOHENLINDEN

On Linden, when the sun was low,
All bloodless lay the untrodden snow ;
And dark as winter was the flow
    Of Iser, rolling rapidly.

But Linden saw another sight,   5
When the drum beat at dead of night
Commanding fires of death to light
    The darkness of her scenery.

69 *fane*, cathedral   72 *sped*, sent quickly
    74 *burghers*, citizens

By torch and trumpet fast array'd
Each horseman drew his battle-blade,   10
And furious every charger neigh'd
        To join the dreadful revelry.

Then shook the hills with thunder riven ;
Then rush'd the steed, to battle driven ;
And louder than the bolts of Heaven   15
        Far flash'd the red artillery.

But redder yet that light shall glow
On Linden's hills of stainéd snow ;
And bloodier yet the torrent flow
        Of Iser, rolling rapidly.   20

'Tis morn ; but scarce yon level sun
Can pierce the war-clouds, rolling dun,
Where furious Frank and fiery Hun
        Shout in their sulphurous canopy.

The combat deepens.   On, ye Brave   25
Who rush to glory, or the grave !
Wave, Munich, all thy banners wave,
        And charge with all thy chivalry !

Few, few shall part, where many meet !
The snow shall be their winding-sheet,   30
And every turf beneath their feet
        Shall be a soldier's sepulchre.

                                    T. Campbell

* 49 *

THE LAST CHARGE OF THE FRENCH AT WATERLOO

ON came the whirlwind—like the last
But fiercest sweep of tempest-blast—
On came the whirlwind—steel-gleams broke
Like lightning through the rolling smoke ;

9 *array'd*, dressed   11 *charger*, war-horse   15 than thunder
16 *artillery*, cannon   22 *dun*, gloomy
24 *sulphurous canopy*, overhanging smoke from guns
28 *chivalry*, horsemen   32 *sepulchre*, grave

The war was waked anew,   5
Three hundred cannon-mouths roar'd loud,
And from their throats, with flash and cloud,
      Their showers of iron threw.
Beneath their fire, in full career,
Rush'd on the ponderous cuirassier,   10
The lancer couch'd his ruthless spear,
And hurrying as to havoc near,
      The cohorts' eagles flew.
In one dark torrent, broad and strong,
The advancing onset roll'd along,   15
Forth harbinger'd by fierce acclaim,
That, from the shroud of smoke and flame,
Peal'd wildly the imperial name !

But on the British heart were lost
The terrors of the charging host ;   20
For not an eye the storm that view'd
Changed its proud glance of fortitude ;
Nor was one forward footstep stay'd,
As dropp'd the dying and the dead.
Fast as their ranks the thunders tear,   25
Fast they renew'd each serried square ;
And on the wounded and the slain
Closed their diminish'd files again,
Till from their line scarce spears' lengths three,
Emerging from the smoke they see   30
Helmet, and plume, and panoply,—
      Then waked their fire at once !
Each musketeer's revolving knell,
As fast, as regularly fell,
As when they practise to display   35
Their discipline on festal day.

10 *cuirassier*, heavily armed horseman
13 *cohort*, body of men   16 *harbinger'd*, preceded
17 *shroud*, covering   18 *name*, Napoleon Buonaparte
22 *fortitude*, bravery   26 *serried*, closely drawn
31 *panoply*, armour   33 firing in turn

Then down went helm and lance,
Down were the eagle-banners sent,
   Down reeling steeds and riders went,
Corslets were pierced, and pennons rent ;   40
   And to augment the fray,
Wheel'd full against their staggering flanks,
The English horsemen's foaming ranks
   Forced their resistless way.
Then to the musket-knell succeeds   45
The clash of swords—the neigh of steeds—
As plies the smith his clanging trade,
Against the cuirass rang the blade ;
And while amid their close array
The well-served cannon rent their way,   50
And while amid their scatter'd band
Raged the fierce rider's bloody brand,
Recoil'd in common rout and fear
Lancer and guard and cuirassier,
Horsemen and foot,—a mingled host !   55
Their leaders fall'n,—their standards lost.

                        Sir W. Scott

* 50 *

THE SOLDIER'S DREAM.

OUR bugles sang truce, for the night-cloud had
    lower'd,
  And the sentinel stars set their watch in the sky ;
And thousands had sunk on the ground overpower'd,
  The weary to sleep, and the wounded to die.

When reposing that night on my pallet of straw   5
  By the wolf-scaring faggot that guarded the slain,
At the dead of the night a sweet Vision I saw ;
  And thrice ere the morning I dreamt it again.

         38 the Eagle was borne by the French
  40 *corslet*, body-armour   41 *augment*, increase
   1 *truce*, peace for the time : *lower'd*, descended
   5 *pallet*, couch   6 fire lighted to keep the wolves away

Methought from the battle-field's dreadful array
   Far, far, I had roam'd on a desolate track :   10
'Twas Autumn,—and sunshine arose on the way
   To the home of my fathers, that welcomed me
     back.

I flew to the pleasant fields traversed so oft
   In life's morning march, when my bosom was
     young ;
I heard my own mountain-goats bleating aloft,   15
   And knew the sweet strain that the corn-reapers
     sung.

Then pledged we the wine-cup, and fondly I swore
   From my home and my weeping friends never to
     part ;
My little ones kiss'd me a thousand times o'er,
   And my wife sobb'd aloud in her fulness of
     heart.   20

' Stay—stay with us !—rest !—thou art weary and
   worn ! '—
   And fain was their war-broken soldier to stay ;—
But sorrow return'd with the dawning of morn,
   And the voice in my dreaming ear melted away.
                           T. Campbell

∗ 51 ∗

BLIND BELISARIUS

HEAVEN'S gifts are unequal in this world awarded,
As the wise page of history to us has recorded ;
Since the learn'd, great, and good, of its frowns
   seldom scape any :—
Witness brave Belisarius, who begg'd for a half-
   penny :—
'*Date obolum, Date obolum, Date obolum, Belisario,*' 5

---

    17 we drank healths   1 *awarded*, given
      5 Give a half-penny to Belisarius

He whose fame from his valour and victories arose,
    sir,
Of his country the shield, and the scourge of her
    foes, sir :
By his poor faithful dog, blind and aged, was led
With one foot in the grave, thus to beg for his bread.

When a young Roman knight, in the street passing
    by,   10
The veteran survey'd with a heart-rending sigh :
His purse in his helmet he dropp'd with a tear,
While the soldier's sad tale thus attracted his ear.

' I have fought, I have bled, I have conquer'd for
    Rome ;
' I have crown'd her with laurels, which for ages shall
    bloom ;   15
  I've enrich'd her with wealth, swell'd her pride and
    her power :
' I espoused her for life,—and disgrace is my dower !

' Yet blood I ne'er wantonly wasted at random,
' Losing thousands their lives by a *nil desperandum :*
' But each conquest I gain'd, I made friend and foe
    know   20
' That my soul's only aim was *pro publico bono.*

' Nor yet for my friends, for my kindred, or self,
' Has my glory been tarnish'd by base views of pelf :
' For such sordid designs I've so far been from
    carving,
' Old and blind, I've no choice, but of begging or
    starving.   25

' Now if soldier or statesman, of what age or nation
' He hereafter may be, should hear this relation,
' And of eyesight bereft, should like me grope his way,
' The bright sun-beams of virtue will turn night to
    day !

11 *veteran*, old soldier   19 rash courage   21 for the public good
23 *pelf*, making money   24 *carving*, contriving   27 *relation*, tale

' But if wanting that light, at the close of life's
    spark,   30
' He at length comes to take the great leap in the
    dark,
' He may wish, while his friends wring their hands
    round his bed,
' That, like poor Belisarius, he'd begg'd for his
    bread.
' But I to distress and to darkness inured,
' In this vile crust of clay when no longer im-
    mured,   35
' At death's welcome stroke my bright course shall
    begin, sir,
' And enjoy endless day from the sunshine within,
    sir :—
' *Date obolum, Date obolum, Date obolum, Belisario.'*
                                     J. Collins

* 52 *

THE FAIRY LIFE

I

WHERE the bee sucks, there suck I :
In a cowslip's bell I lie ;
There I couch, when owls do cry :
On the bat's back I do fly
After summer merrily.   5
    Merrily, merrily, shall I live now,
    Under the blossom that hangs on the bough.

II

COME unto these yellow sands,
    And then take hands :
Courtsied when you have and kiss'd
    The wild waves whist,

---

31 *to* die   34 *inured*, accustomed   35 *crust*, his body :
                       immured, built up

Foot it featly here and there ;   5
And, sweet sprites, the burthen bear.
     Hark, hark !
        Bow-wow.
     The watch-dog's bark :
        Bow-wow.   10
Hark, hark ! I hear
The strain of strutting chanticleer
Cry, Cock-a-diddle-dow !

                       W. Shakespeare

* 53 *

THE FAIRIES

UP the airy mountain,
  Down the rushy glen,
We daren't go a-hunting
  For fear of little men ;
Wee folk, good folk,   5
  Trooping all together ;
Green jacket, red cap,
  And white owl's feather !

Down along the rocky shore
  Some make their home :   10
They live on crispy pancakes
  Of yellow tide-foam ;
Some in the reeds
  Of the black mountain lake,
With frogs for their watch-dogs,   15
  All night awake.

High on the hill-top
  The old King sits ;
He is now so old and gray,
  He's nigh lost his wits.   20
With a bridge of white mist
  Columbkill he crosses,

On his stately journeys
  From Slieveleague to Rosses :—
Or going up with music   25
  On cold starry nights,
To sup with the queen
  Of the gay Northern Lights.

They stole little Bridget
  For seven years long ;   30
When she came down again,
  Her friends were all gone.

They took her lightly back,
  Between the night and morrow ;
They thought that she was fast asleep,   35
  But she was dead with sorrow.
They have kept her ever since
  Deep within the lakes,
On a bed of flag-leaves,
  Watching till she wakes.   40

By the craggy hill-side,
  Through the mosses bare,
They have planted thorn-trees
  For pleasure here and there.
Is any man so daring   45
  As dig them up in spite,
He shall find their sharpest thorns
  In his bed at night.

Up the airy mountain,
  Down the rushy glen,   50
We daren't go a-hunting
  For fear of little men ;
Wee folk, good folk,
  Trooping all together ;
Green jacket, red cap,   55
  And white owl's feather !

W. Allingham

• 54 •

THE WIFE OF USHER'S WELL

THERE lived a wife at Usher's Well,
  And a wealthy wife was she :
She had three stout and stalwart sons,
  And sent them o'er the sea.

They had not been a week from her,   5
  A week but barely ane,
When word came to the carline wife
  That her three sons were gane.

They had not been a week from her,
  A week but barely three,   10
When word came to the carline wife
  That her sons she'd never see.

' I wish the wind may never cease,
  ' Nor fishes in the flood,
' Till my three sons come hame to me,   15
  ' In earthly flesh and blood ! '·

It fell about the Martinmas,
  When nights are lang and mirk,
The carline wife's three sons came home,
  And their hats were of the birk.   20

It neither grew in syke nor ditch,
  Nor yet in ony sheugh ;
But at the gates of Paradise
  That birk grew fair eneugh.

' Blow up the fire, my maidens !   25
  ' Bring water from the well !
' For all my house shall feast this night,
  ' Since my three sons are well ! '

---

7 *carline*, old peasant-woman   18 *mirk*, murky
20 *birk*, birch   21 *syke*, marsh   22 *sheugh*, trench

And she has made to them a bed,
   She's made it large and wide ;   30
And she's ta'en her mantle her about ;
   Sat down at the bed-side.

Up then crew the red, red cock,
   And up and crew the gray :
The eldest to the youngest said,   35
   ''Tis time we were away !

' The cock doth craw, the day doth daw,
   ' The channerin' worm doth chide :
' If we be miss'd out of our place,
   ' A sore pain we must bide.   40

' Fare ye well, my mother dear !
   ' Farewell to barn and byre !
'And fare ye well, the bonny lass,
   ' That kindles my mother's fire !'
                          Unknown

* 55 *

ALICE BRAND

I

MERRY it is in the good greenwood,
   When the mavis and merle are singing,
When the deer sweeps by, and the hounds are in
      cry,
   And the hunter's horn is ringing.

' O Alice Brand, my native land   5
   ' Is lost for love of you ;
' And we must hold by wood and wold,
   ' As outlaws wont to do !

37 *daw*, dawn   38 *channerin'*, scolding : probably here, impatient
42 *byre*, cattle-house   2 *mavis*, thrush : *merle*, blackbird

'O Alice, 'twas all for thy locks so bright,
  'And 'twas all for thine eyes so blue,   10
'That on the night of our luckless flight,
  'Thy brother bold I slew.

'Now must I teach to hew the beech,
  'The hand that held the glaive,
'For leaves to spread our lowly bed,   15
  'And stakes to fence our cave.

'And for vest of pall, thy fingers small,
  'That wont on harp to stray,
'A cloak must shear from the slaughter'd deer,
  'To keep the cold away.'—   20

—'O Richard ! if my brother died,
  ''Twas but a fatal chance :
'For darkling was the battle tried,
  'And fortune sped the lance.

'If pall and vair no more I wear,   25
  'Nor thou the crimson sheen,
'As warm, we'll say, is the russet gray ;
  'As gay the forest-green.

'And, Richard, if our lot be hard,
  'And lost thy native land,   30
'Still Alice has her own Richárd,
  'And he his Alice Brand.'

II

'Tis merry, 'tis merry, in good greenwood,
  So blithe Lady Alice is singing ;
On the beech's pride, and oak's brown side,
  Lord Richard's axe is ringing.

---

14 *glaive*, broad-sword   16 *pall*, fine cloth
24 *sped*, directed   25 *vair*, fur   35 the lofty beech

Up spoke the moody Elfin King,
   Who wonn'd within the hill,—
Like wind in the porch of a ruin'd church,
   His voice was ghostly shrill.   40

' Why sounds yon stroke on beech and oak,
   ' Our moonlight circle's screen ?
' Or who comes here to chase the deer,
   ' Beloved of our Elfin Queen ?
' Or who may dare on wold to wear   45
   ' The fairies' fatal green ?

' Up, Urgan, up ! to yon mortal hie,
   ' For thou wert christen'd man :
' For cross or sign thou wilt not fly,
   ' For mutter'd word or ban.   50

' Lay on him the curse of the wither'd heart,
   ' The curse of the sleepless eye ;
' Till he wish and pray that his life would part,
   ' Nor yet find leave to die !'

III

'Tis merry, 'tis merry, in good greenwood,   55
   Though the birds have still'd their singing ;
The evening blaze doth Alice raise,
   And Richard is fagots bringing.

Up Urgan starts, that hideous dwarf,
   Before Lord Richard stands,   60
And as he cross'd and bless'd himself,
' I fear not sign,' quoth the grisly elf,
   ' That is made with bloody hands.'

But out then spoke she, Alice Brand,
   That woman void of fear,—   65
' And if there's blood upon his hand,
   ' 'Tis but the blood of deer.'

37 *Elfin*, fairy   38 *wonn'd*, dwelt   47 *mortal*, man   50 *ban*, curse

—'Now loud thou liest, thou bold of mood !
 'It cleaves unto his hand,
'The stain of thine own kindly blood, 70
 'The blood of Ethert Brand.'

Then forward stepp'd she, Alice Brand,
 And made the holy sign,—
'And if there's blood on Richard's hand,
 'A spotless hand is mine. 75

'And I conjure thee, Demon elf,
 'By Him whom Demons fear,
'To show us whence thou art thyself,
 'And what thine errand here ?'

IV

—''Tis merry, 'tis merry, in Fairy-land, 80
 'When fairy birds are singing,
'When the court doth ride by their monarch's side,
 'With bit and bridle ringing :

'And gaily shines the Fairy land—
 'But all is glistening show, 85
'Like the idle gleam that December's beam
 'Can dart on ice and snow.

'And fading, like that varied gleam,
 'Is our inconstant shape,
'Who now like knight and lady seem, 90
 'And now like dwarf and ape.

'It was between the night and day,
 'When the Fairy King has power,
'That I sunk down in a sinful fray,
'And 'twixt life and death, was snatch'd away 95
 'To the joyless Elfin bower.

76 *conjure*, order 89 *inconstant*, changeable 94 *fray*, quarrel

'But wist I of a woman bold,
  'Who thrice my brow durst sign,
'I might regain my mortal mould,
  'As fair a form as thine.'   100

She cross'd him once—she cross'd him twice—
  That lady was so brave ;
The fouler grew his goblin hue,
  The darker grew the cave.

She cross'd him thrice, that lady bold !   105
  —He rose beneath her hand
The fairest knight on Scottish mould,
  Her brother, Ethert Brand !

—Merry it is in good greenwood,
  When the mavis and merle are singing ;   110
But merrier were they in Dunfermline gray
  When all the bells were ringing.

                                   Sir W. Scott

* 56 *

KUBLA KHAN

A Vision in a Dream

IN Xanadu did Kubla Khan
A stately pleasure-dome decree :
Where Alph, the sacred river, ran
Through caverns measureless to man
      Down to a sunless sea.   5
So twice five miles of fertile ground
With walls and towers were girdled round :
And there were gardens bright with sinuous rills
Where blossom'd many an incense-bearing tree ;
And here were forests ancient as the hills,   10
Enfolding sunny spots of greenery.

----

97 *wist*, knew   2 *decree*, order to be built
          8 *sinuous*, winding

But oh ! that deep romantic chasm which slanted
Down the green hill athwart a cedarn cover !
A savage place ! as holy and enchanted
As e'er beneath a waning moon was haunted   15
By woman wailing for her demon-lover !
And from this chasm, with ceaseless turmoil
    seething,
As if this earth in fast thick pants were breathing,
A mighty fountain momently was forced :
Amid whose swift half-intermitted burst   20
Huge fragments vaulted like rebounding hail,
Or chaffy grain beneath the thresher's flail ;
And 'mid these dancing rocks at once and ever
It flung up momently the sacred river.
Five miles meandering with a mazy motion   25
Through wood and dale the sacred river ran,
Then reach'd the caverns measureless to man,
And sank in tumult to a lifeless ocean :
And 'mid this tumult Kubla heard from far
Ancestral voices prophesying war !   30

    The shadow of the dome of pleasure
    Floated midway on the waves ;
    Where was heard the mingled measure
    From the fountain and the caves.
It was a miracle of rare device,   35
A sunny pleasure-dome with caves of ice ;
    A damsel with a dulcimer
    In a vision once I saw :
    It was an Abyssinian maid,
    And on her dulcimer she play'd,   40
    Singing of Mount Abora !
    Could I revive within me
    Her symphony and song,

12 *chasm*, sharp hollow

13 *cedarn*, of cedars	19 *momently*, every moment
20 *intermitted*, stopping	25 *meandering*, winding
30 voices of his forefathers	33 *measure*, song
37 *dulcimer*, guitar	43 *symphony*, accompaniment

To such a deep delight 'twould win me
That with music loud and long,   45
I would build that dome in air,
That sunny dome !   Those caves of ice !
And all who heard should see them there,
And all should cry Beware ! Beware !
His flashing eyes, his floating hair !   50
Weave a circle round him thrice,
And close your eyes with holy dread,
For he on honey-dew hath fed,
And drunk the milk of Paradise !

                              S. T. Coleridge

* 57 *

THE ECHOING GREEN

THE sun does arise
And make happy the skies ;
The merry bells ring
To welcome the spring ;
The skylark and thrush,   5
The birds of the bush,
Sing louder around
To the bells' cheerful sound ;
While our sports shall be seen
On the echoing green.   10

Old John, with white hair,
Does laugh away care,
Sitting under the oak,
Among the old folk.
They laugh at our play,   15
And soon they all say,
' Such, such were the joys
' When we all—girls and boys—
' In our youth-time were seen

Till the little ones, weary,
No more can be merry ;
The sun does descend,
And our sports have an end.
Round the laps of their mothers   25
Many sisters and brothers,
Like birds in their nest,
Are ready for rest,
And sport no more seen
On the darkening green.   30

W. Blake

* 58 *

A CRADLE SONG

SLEEP, sleep, beauty bright,
Dreaming in the joys of night ;
Sleep, sleep ; in thy sleep
Little sorrows sit and weep.

Sweet babe, in thy face   5
Soft desires I can trace,
Secret joys and secret smiles,
Little pretty infant wiles.

As thy softest limbs I feel,
Smiles as of the morning steal   10
O'er thy cheek, and o'er thy breast
Where thy little heart doth rest.

Oh the cunning wiles that creep
In thy little heart asleep !
When thy little heart doth wake,   15
Then the dreadful light shall break.

W. Blake

8 *wiles*, tricks   16 *light*, knowledge of life with its dangers
and sufferings.

* 59 *

THE ORPHAN CHILDREN

I REACH'D the village on the plain,
   Just when the setting sun's last ray
Shone blazing on the golden vane
   Of the old church across the way.

Across the way alone I sped,   5
   And climb'd the stile, and sat me there,
To think in silence on the dead
   Who in the churchyard sleeping were.

There many a long, low grave I view'd
   Where toil and want in quiet lie ;   10
And costly slabs amongst them stood
   That bore the names of rich and high.

One new made mound I saw close by,
   O'er which the grasses hardly crept,
Where, looking forth with listless eye,   15
   Two ragged children sat and wept.

A piece of bread between them lay,
   Which neither seem'd as it could take ;
And yet so worn and white were they
   With want, it made my bosom ache.   20

I look'd a while, and said at last,
   ' Why in such sorrow sit you here ?
' And why the food you leave and waste
   ' Which your own hunger well might cheer ?'

The boy rose instant to his feet,   25
   And said with gentle, eager haste,
' Lady, we've not enough to eat :
   ' O if we had, we should not waste !

' But sister Mary's naughty grown.
   ' And will not eat, whate'er I say ;   30
' Though sure I am the bread 's her own,
   ' For she has tasted none to-day !'

' Indeed,' the poor starved Mary said,
  ' Till Henry eats, I'll eat no more ;
' For yesterday I had some bread ;   35
  ' He's had none since the day before.'

My heart with pity swell'd so high
  I could not speak a single word :
Yet the boy straightway made reply,
  As if my inward wish he heard.   40

' Before our father went away,
  ' By bad men tempted o'er the sea,
' Sister and I did nought but play ;—
  ' We lived beside yon great ash-tree.

' But then poor mother did so cry,   45
  ' And look'd so changed, I cannot tell !
' She told us that she soon should die,
  ' And bade us love each other well.

' She said that when the war was o'er,
  ' Perhaps our father we might see :   50
' But if we never saw him more,
  ' That God would then our father be.

' She kiss'd us both, and then she died,
  ' And then they put her in the grave :
' There many a day we've sat and cried   55
  ' That we no more a mother have.

' But when our father came not here,
  ' I thought if we could find the sea
' We should be sure to meet him there,
  ' And once again might happy be.   60

' So hand-in-hand for many a mile,
  ' And many a long, long day we went :
' Some sigh'd to see, some turn'd to smile,
  ' And fed us when our stock was spent.

' But when we reach'd the sea, and found   65
 ' 'Twas one great flood before us spread,
' We thought that father must be drown'd,
 ' And cried, and wish'd we too were dead.

' So we came back to mother's grave,
 ' And only long with her to be :   70
' For Goody, when this bread she gave,
 ' Said father died beyond the sea.

' So, since no parent we have here,
 ' We'll go and search for God around :—
' Pray, Lady, can you tell us where   75
 ' That God, our Father, may be found?

' He lives in heaven, mother said :
 ' And Goody says that mother 's there :
' But though we've walk'd, and search'd, and pray'd,
 ' We cannot find them anywhere !'   80

I clasp'd the prattlers in my arms,
 I cried, ' Come, both, and live with me !
' I'll clothe and feed you, safe from harms —
 ' Your second mother I will be.

' Till you to your own mother's side   85
 ' He in his own good time may call,
' With Him for ever to abide
 ' Who is the Father of us all !'

          Unknown

* 60 *

THE CHILD AND THE MOWERS

Dorset Dialect

O, AYE ! they had woone chile bezide,
 An' a finer your eyes never met ;
'Twer a dear little fellow that died
 In the zummer that come wi' such het ;

---

 1 *woone*, one   3 *'Twer*, it was   4 *het*, heat

By the mowers, too thoughtless in fun,   5
  He wer then a-zent off vrom our eyes,
Vrom the light ov the dew-dryèn zun,—
  Aye ! vrom days under blue-hollow'd skies.

He went out to the mowers in meäd,
  When the zun wer a-rose to his height,   10
An' the men wer a-swingèn the sneäd,
  Wi' their eärms in white sleeves, left an' right :--
An' out there, as they rested at noon,
  O ! they drench'd en wi' eäle-horns too deep,
Till his thoughts wer a-drown'd in a swoon ;   15
  Aye! his life wer a-smother'd in sleep.

Then they laid en there-right on the ground,
  On a grass-heap, a-zweltrèn wi' het,
Wi' his heäir all a-wetted around
  His young feäce, wi' the big drops o' zweat ;   20
In his little left palm he'd a-zet
  Wi' his right hand, his vore-vinger's tip,
As for zome'hat he woulden forget,—
  Aye ! zome thought that he woulden let slip.

Then they took en in hwome to his bed,   25
  An' he rose vrom his pillow noo mwore,
Vor the curls on his sleek little head
  To be blown by the wind out o' door.
Vor he died while the häy russled gray
  On the staddle so leätely begun,   30
Lik' the mown-grass a-dried by the day,—
  Aye ! the zwath-flow'r's a-kill'd by the zun.

W. Barnes

6 *a-zent*, sent   7 *dryen*, drying   9 *in mead*, in the meadow
11 *snead*, handle of scythe   14 *en*, him : *eäle-horns*, full of ale
18 *a-zweltren*, sweltering   21 *a-zet*, put
   23 *zome'hat*, something : *woulden*, would not
   26 *noo mwore*, no more
   30 *staddle*, platform on which the rick stands
   32 *zwath-flower*, cut down with the swath

* 61 *

ELLEN BRINE OF ALLENBURN

Dorset dialect

Noo soul did hear her lips complaïn,
An' she's a-gone vrom all her païn,
An' others' loss to her is gain
For she do live in heaven's love ;
Vull many a longsome day an' week   5
She bore her aïlèn, still, an' meek ;
A-workèn while her strangth held on,
An' guidèn housework, when 'twer gone.
    Vor Ellen Brine of Allenburn
    Oh! there be souls to murn.   10

The last time I'd a-cast my zight
·Upon her feäce, a-feäded white,
Wer in a zummer's mornèn light
In hall avore the smwold'rèn vire,
The while the childern beät the vloor   15
In playÿ, wi' tiny shoes they wore,
An' call'd their mother's eyes to view
The feäts their little limbs could do.
    Oh! Ellen Brine of Allenburn,
    They childern now mus' murn.   20

Then woone, a-stoppèn vrom his reäce,
Went up, an' on her knee did pleäce
His hand, a-lookèn in her feäce,
An' wi' a smilèn mouth so small,
He zaid, 'You promised us to goo   25
' To Shroton feäir, an' teäke us two!'

2 *an'*, and : *vrom*, from : *v* used for *f* in Dorset
6 *aïlen*, illness   7 *a-worken*, working   10 *murn*, mourn
12 *feaded*, faded   14 *avore*, before : *smwold'ren*, smouldering
21 *woone*, one : *reace*, running

She heärd it wi' her two white cars,
An' in her eyes there sprung two tears :—
   Vor Ellen Brine of Allenburn
   Did veel that they mus' murn.   30

September come, wi' Shroton feäir,
But Ellen Brine wer never there !
A heavy heart wer on the meäre
Their father rod his hwomeward road.
'Tis true he brought some feärèns back,   35
Vor them two childern all in black ;
But they had now, wi' plaÿthings new,
Noo mother vor to show em to :—
   Vor Ellen Brine of Allenburn
   Would never mwore return.   40
                             W. Barnes

* 62 *

HELVELLYN

I CLIMB'D the dark brow of the mighty Helvellyn,
   Lakes and mountains beneath me gleam'd misty
      and wide ;
All was still, save by fits, when the eagle was yelling,
   And starting around me the echoes replied.
On the right, Striden-edge round the Red-tarn was
      bending,   5
And Catchedicam its left verge was defending,
One huge nameless rock in the front was ascending,
   When I mark'd the sad spot where the wanderer
      had died.

Dark green was that spot 'mid the brown mountain
      heather,
   Where the Pilgrim of Nature lay stretch'd in
      decay,   10

---

33 *meare*, mare   35 *feärèns*, fairings
1 *brow*, mountain-side   3 *by fits*, now and then
      6 *verge*, edge : *defending*, sheltering
10 *Pilgrim*, wanderer who admired the natural landscape

Like the corpse of an outcast abandon'd to weather
  Till the mountain-winds wasted the tenantless clay.
Nor yet quite deserted, though lonely extended,
For, faithful in death, his mute favourite attended,
The much-loved remains of her master defended, 15
  And chased the hill-fox and the raven away.

How long didst thou think that his silence was
    slumber?
  When the wind waved his garment, how oft didst
    thou start?
How many long days and long weeks didst thou
    number,
  Ere he faded before thee, the friend of thy
    heart?   20
And, oh! was it meet, that—no requiem read o'er
    him—
No mother to weep, and no friend to deplore him,
And thou, little guardian, alone stretch'd before
    him—
  Unhonour'd the Pilgrim from life should depart?

When a Prince to the fate of the Peasant has
    yielded,   25
  The tapestry waves dark round the dim-lighted
    hall;
With scutcheons of silver the coffin is shielded,
  And pages stand mute by the canopied pall:
Through the courts, at deep midnight, the torches
    are gleaming;
In the proudly-arch'd chapel the banners are beam-
    ing;   30
Far adown the long aisle sacred music is streaming,
  Lamenting a Chief of the People should fall.

12 *tenantless clay*, body without soul   13 *extended*, stretched out
       14 *mute favourite*, speechless dog
   21 *meet*, fit: *requiem*, funeral service   25 has died
   26 *tapestry*, rich hangings on walls   27 *scutcheons*, shields
       28 *pages*, servants: *canopied*, covered

But meeter for thee, gentle lover of nature,
  To lay down thy head like the meek mountain
     lamb,
When, wilder'd, he drops from some cliff huge in
     stature,   35
  And draws his last sob by the side of his dam.
And more stately thy couch by this desert lake lying,
Thy obsequies sung by the gray plover flying,
With one faithful friend but to witness thy dying,
  In the arms of Helvellyn and Catchedicam.   40

Sir W. Scott

* 63 *

A REVERIE

WHEN, musing on companions gone,
We doubly feel ourselves alone,
Something, my Friend, we yet may gain ;
There is a pleasure in this pain :
It soothes the love of lonely rest,   5
Deep in each gentler heart impress'd.
'Tis silent amid worldly toils,
And stifled soon by mental broils ;
But, in a bosom thus prepared,
Its still small voice is often heard,   10
Whispering a mingled sentiment,
'Twixt resignation and content.

Oft in my mind such thoughts awake,
By lone Saint Mary's silent lake ;
Thou know'st it well,—nor fen, nor sedge, 15
Pollute the pure lake's crystal edge ;
Abrupt and sheer, the mountains sink
At once upon the level brink ;
And just a trace of silver sand
  Marks where the water meets the land.   20

---

33 *meeter*, fitter   38 *obsequies*, funeral service   40 surrounded by
1 *musing*, thinking   6 *impressed*, stamped   8 by troubles of
the mind   16 *pollute*, spoil   17 going straight up

Far in the mirror, bright and blue,
Each hill's huge outline you may view ;
Shaggy with heath, but lonely bare,
Nor tree, nor bush, nor brake, is there,
Save where, of land, yon slender line   25
Bears thwart the lake the scatter'd pine.
Yet even this nakedness has power,
And aids the feeling of the hour :
Nor thicket, dell, nor copse you spy,
Where living thing conceal'd might lie ;   30
Nor point, retiring, hides a dell,
Where swain, or woodman lone, might dwell ;
There's nothing left to fancy's guess,
You see that all is loneliness :
And silence aids—though the steep hills   35
Send to the lake a thousand rills ;
In summer-tide, so soft they weep,
The sound but lulls the ear asleep ;
Your horse's hoof-tread sounds too rude,
So stilly is the solitude.   40

Sir W. Scott

* 64 *

SUCH IS LIFE

LIKE to the falling of a star,
Or as the flights of eagles are,
Or like the fresh Spring's gaudy hue,
Or silver drops of morning dew ;
Or like a wind that chafes the flood,   5
Or bubbles which on water stood ;—
E'en such is man, whose borrow'd light
Is straight call'd in and paid to-night.
The wind blows out, the bubble dies,
The Spring entomb'd in Autumn lies ;   10
The dew dries up, the star is shot,
The flight is past ;—and Man forgot.

Bishop King

26 *thwart*, crossing   36 *rills*, little streams   10 *entomb'd*, buried

* 65 *

JOHN ANDERSON

JOHN ANDERSON my jo, John,
When we were first acquent
Your locks were like the raven,
Your bonnie brow was brent ;
But now your brow is bald, John,   5
Your locks are like the snow ;
But blessings on your frosty pow,
John Anderson my jo.

John Anderson my jo, John,
We clamb the hill thegither,   10
And mony a canty day, John,
We've had wi' ane anither :
Now we maun totter down, John,
But hand in hand we'll go,
And sleep thegither at the foot,   15
John Anderson my jo.

R. Burns

* 66 *

A LESSON

THERE is a flower, the Lesser Celandine,
That shrinks like many more from cold and rain,
And the first moment that the sun may shine,
Bright as the sun himself, 'tis out again !

When hailstones have been falling, swarm on
    swarm,   5
Or blasts the green field and the trees distrest,
Oft have I seen it muffled up from harm
In close self-shelter, like a thing at rest.

1 *jo,* love	2 *acquent,* acquainted	4 *brent,* smooth
7 *pow,* head	10 *thegither,* together	11 *canty,* cheerful
	13 *maun,* must	

But lately, one rough day, this flower I past,
And recognized it, though an alter'd form,   10
Now standing forth an offering to the blast,
And buffeted at will by rain and storm.

I stopp'd and said, with inly-mutter'd voice,
' It doth not love the shower, nor seek the cold ;
' This neither is its courage nor its choice,   15
' But its necessity in being old.

' The sunshine may not cheer it, nor the dew ;
' It cannot help itself in its decay ;
' Stiff in its members, wither'd, changed of hue,'
And, in my spleen, I smiled that it was gray.   20

To be a prodigal's favourite—then, worse truth,
A miser's pensioner—behold our lot !
O Man ! that from thy fair and shining youth
Age might but take the things Youth needed not !
                                    W. Wordsworth

* 67 *

TRUE GROWTH

IT is not growing like a tree
In bulk, doth make Man better be ;
Or standing long an oak, three hundred year,
To fall a log at last, dry, bald, and sere :
        A lily of a day   5
        Is fairer far in May,
Although it fall and die that night—
It was the plant and flower of Light !
In small proportions we just beauties see ;
And in short measures life may perfect be.   10
                                    B. Jonson

21 *a prodigal's favourite*, wasting the many gifts of Youth
22 *a miser's pensioner*, getting the little we can from Age
        9 *just*, true

* 68 *

FLOWERS WITHOUT FRUIT

PRUNE thou thy words ; the thoughts control
   That o'er thee swell and throng :—
They will condense within thy soul,
   And change to purpose strong.

But he who lets his feelings run   5
   In soft luxurious flow,
Shrinks when hard service must be done,
   And faints at every woe.

Faith's meanest deed more favour bears,
   Where hearts and wills are weigh'd,   10
Than brightest transports, choicest prayers,
   Which bloom their hour, and fade.
                J. H. Newman

* 69 *

CONTENTMENT

MY mind to me a kingdom is ;
   Such perfect joy therein I find,
As far exceeds all earthly bliss
   That world affords, or grows by kind :
Though much I want what most men have,   5
Yet doth my mind forbid me crave.

Content I live—this is my stay ;
   I seek no more than may suffice :
I press to bear no haughty sway ;
   Look—what I lack, my mind supplies !   10
Lo ! thus I triumph like a king,
Content with that my mind doth bring.

      3 *condense*, grow close and strong
     4 *by kind*, naturally .   6 *crave*, desire
7 *stay*, support   8 *suffice*, be enough   9 *press*, strive

I see how plenty surfeits oft,
   And hasty climbers soonest fall ;
I see how those that sit aloft   15
   Mishap doth threaten most of all ;
These get with toil, and keep with fear :
Such cares my mind could never bear.

I laugh not at another's loss ;
   I grudge not at another's gain ;   20
No worldly wave my mind can toss ;
   I brook that is another's pain.
I fear no foe : I scorn no friend :
I dread no death : I fear no end.

Some have too much, yet still they crave ; 25
   I little have, yet seek no more :
They are but poor, though much they have,
   And I am rich, with little store.
They poor, I rich : they beg, I give :
They lack, I lend : they pine, I live.   30

I wish but what I have at will :
   I wander not to seek for more :
I like the plain ; I climb no hill :
   In greatest storm I sit on shore,
And laugh at those that toil in vain,   35
To get what must be lost again.
—This is my choice ; for why?—I find
No wealth is like a quiet mind.

                   Sir E. Dyer

* 70 *

THE SEARCH FOR PEACE

Sweet Peace, where dost thou dwell? I humbly
    crave,
      Let me once know.
   I sought thee in a secret cave,
     And ask'd, if Peace were there ?

13 *surfeits*, sickens   22 *brook that*, bear easily what
31 *at will*, at command   1 *crave*, beg to know

A hollow wind did seem to answer, ' No :—   5
   ' Go seek elsewhere.'

I did ; and going did a rainbow note :
      Surely, thought I,
   This is the lace of Peace's coat :
     I will search out the matter.   10
But while I look'd, the clouds immediately
    Did break and scatter.

Then went I to a garden, and did spy
      A gallant flower,
   The Crown Imperial : Sure, said I,   15
     Peace at the root must dwell.
But when I digg'd, I saw a worm devour
    What show'd so well.

At length I met a reverend good old man :
      Whom when for Peace   20
   I did demand, he thus began :
     ' There was a Prince of old
' At Salem dwelt, who lived with good increase
    ' Of flock and fold.

' He sweetly lived ; yet sweetness did not save   25
      ' His life from foes.
   ' But after death, out of his grave
     ' There sprang twelve stalks of wheat :
' Which many wondering at, got some of those
    ' To plant and set.   30

' It prosper'd strangely, and did soon disperse
      ' Through all the earth :
   ' For they that taste it do rehearse,
     ' That virtue lies therein ;
' A secret virtue, bringing peace and mirth   35
    ' By flight of sin.

31 *it*, the Gospel   33 *rehearse*, say   35 *virtue*, power

Take of this grain, which in my garden grows,
 'And grows for you ;
 'Make bread of it :—and that repose
  'And peace, which everywhere   40
With so much earnestness you do pursue,
  'Is only there.'

G. Herbert

* 7 1 *

THE KITTEN AND FALLING LEAVES.

THAT way look, my Infant, lo !
What a pretty baby-show !
See the Kitten on the wall,
Sporting with the leaves that fall,
Wither'd leaves—one—two—and three— 5
From the lofty elder-tree !
Through the calm and frosty air
Of this morning bright and fair,
Eddying round and round they sink
Softly, slowly : one might think, 10
From the motions that are made,
Every little leaf convey'd
Sylph or Faery hither tending,—
To this lower world descending,
Each invisible and mute, 15
In his wavering parachute.
——But the Kitten, how she starts,
Crouches, stretches, paws, and darts !
First at one, and then its fellow
Just as light and just as yellow ; 20
There are many now—now one—
Now they stop, and there are none :
What intenseness of desire
In her upward eye of fire !

9 *eddying*, turning 13 *Sylph*, learned name for fairy
16 *parachute*, machine to float slowly down in the air
23 *intenseness*, strength

With a tiger-leap half way   25
Now she meets the coming prey,
Lets it go as fast, and then
Has it in her power again :
Now she works with three or four,
Like an Indian conjuror ;   30
Quick as he in feats of art,
Far beyond in joy of heart.
Were her antics play'd in th' eye
Of a thousand standers-by,
Clapping hands with shout and stare,   35
What would little Tabby care
For the plaudits of the crowd ?
Over happy to be proud,
Over wealthy in the treasure
Of her own exceeding pleasure !   40
    'Tis a pretty baby-treat ;
Nor, I deem, for me unmeet ;
Here, for neither Babe nor me,
Other play-mate can I see.
Of the countless living things,   45
That with stir of feet and wings
(In the sun or under shade,
Upon bough or grassy blade)
And with busy revellings,
Chirp and song, and murmurings,   50
Made this orchard's narrow space
And this vale so blithe a place,—
Multitudes are swept away
Never more to breathe the day :
Some are sleeping : some in bands   55
Travell'd into distant lands ;
Others slunk to moor and wood,
Far from human neighbourhood ;
And, among the Kinds that keep   _
With us closer fellowship,   60

31 *feats*, tricks   37 *plaudits*, shouts   42 *unmeet*, unfit

With us openly abide,
All have laid their mirth aside.
   Where is he that giddy Sprite,
Blue-cap, with his colours bright,
Who was blest as bird could be,   65
Feeding in the apple-tree ;
Made such wanton spoil and rout,
Turning blossoms inside out ;
Hung—head pointing towards the ground—
Flutter'd, perch'd, into a round   70
Bound himself, and then unbound ;
Lithest, gaudiest Harlequin !
Prettiest Tumbler ever seen !
Light of heart and light of limb ;
What is now become of Him ?   75
Lambs, that through the mountains went
Frisking, bleating merriment,
When the year was in its prime,
They are sober'd by this time.
If you look to vale or hill,   80
If you listen, all is still,
Save a little neighbouring rill,
That from out the rocky ground
Strikes a solitary sound.
Vainly glitter hill and plain,   85
And the air is calm in vain ;
Vainly Morning spreads the lure
Of a sky serene and pure ;
Creature none can she decoy
Into open sign of joy :   90
Is it that they have a fear
Of the dreary season near ?
Or that other pleasures be
Sweeter e'en than gaiety ?
   Yet, whate'er enjoyments dwell   95

87 Morning in vain tempts   89 *decoy*, tempt

In the impenetrable cell
Of the silent heart which Nature
Furnishes to every creature ;
Whatsoe'er we feel and know
Too sedate for outward show, 100
Such a light of gladness breaks,
Pretty Kitten ! from thy freaks, -
Spreads with such a living grace
O'er my little Dora's face ;
Yes, the sight so stirs and charms 105
Thee, Baby, laughing in my arms,
That almost I could repine
That your transports are not mine,
That I do not wholly fare
Even as ye do, thoughtless pair ! 110
And I will have my careless season,
Spite of melancholy reason ;
Will walk through life in such a way
That, when time brings on decay,
Now and then I may possess 115
Hours of perfect gladsomeness.
—Pleased by any random toy ;
By a kitten's busy joy,
Or an infant's laughing eye
Sharing in the ecstasy ; 120
I would fare like that or this,
Find my wisdom in my bliss ;
Keep the sprightly soul awake ;
And have faculties to take,
Even from things by sorrow wrought, 125
Matter for a jocund thought ;
Spite of care, and spite of grief,
To gambol with Life's falling Leaf.

     W. Wordsworth

6, 97 We cannot look into the hearts of living creatures
 100 *sedate*, saddening 107 *repine*, regret
 108 *transports*, delights 124 *faculties*, powers

* 72 *

A SONG OF PRAISE

To God, ye choir above, begin
  A hymn so loud and strong
That all the universe may hear
  And join the grateful song.

Praise Him, thou sun, Who dwells unseen   5
  Amidst transcendent light,
Where thy refulgent orb would seem
  A spot, as dark as night.

Thou silver moon, ye host of stars,
  The universal song   10
Through the serene and silent night
  To listening worlds prolong.

Sing Him, ye distant worlds and suns,
  From whence no travelling ray
Hath yet to us, through ages past,   15
  Had time to make its way.

Assist, ye raging storms, and bear
  On rapid wings His praise,
From north to south, from east to west,
  Through heaven, and earth, and seas.   20

Exert your voice, ye furious fires
  That rend the watery cloud,
And thunder to this nether world
  Your Maker's words aloud.

Ye works of God, that dwell unknown   25
  Beneath the rolling main ;
Ye birds, that sing among the groves,
  And sweep the azure plain ;

1 *choir*, all Nature   6 *transcendent*, surpassingly bright
7 *refulgent*, shining   11 *serene*, clear
13 stars so distant that their light has not yet reached us
21 *fires*, lightnings   23 *nether*, lower   28 the sky

Ye stately hills, that rear your heads,
  And towering pierce the sky ;   30
Ye clouds, that with an awful pace
  Majestic roll on high ;

Ye insects small, to which one leaf
  Within its narrow sides
A vast extended world displays,   35
  And spacious realms provides ;

Ye race, still less than these, with which
  The stagnant water teems,
To which one drop, however small,
  A boundless ocean seems ;   40

Whate'er ye are, where'er ye dwell,
  Ye creatures great or small,
Adore the wisdom, praise the power,
  That made and governs all.

                 P. Skelton

* 73 *

THE SONG OF DAVID

HE sang of God, the mighty source
Of all things, the stupendous force
  On which all strength depends ;
From whose right arm, beneath whose eyes,
All period, power, and enterprize   5
  Commences, reigns, and ends.

The world, the clustering spheres he made,
The glorious light, the soothing shade,
  Dale, champaign, grove, and hill :
The multitudinous abyss,   10
Where secresy remains in bliss,
  And wisdom hides her skill.

7 *spheres*, stars   9 *champaign*, level country
       10 *abyss*, space

Tell them, I AM, Jehovah said
To Moses : while Earth heard in dread,
   And, smitten to the heart,   15
At once, above, beneath, around,
All Nature, without voice, or sound,
   Replied, 'O Lord, THOU ART.'

                    C. Smart

* 74 *

THE TRAVELLER

How are thy servants blest, O Lord !
   How sure is their defence !
Eternal wisdom is their guide,
   Their help, Omnipotence.

In foreign realms, and lands remote,   5
   Supported by Thy care,
Through burning climes I pass'd unhurt,
   And breathed in tainted air.

Thy mercy sweeten'd every soil,
   Made every region please ;   10
The hoary Alpine hills it warm'd,
   And smoothed the Tyrrhene seas.

Think, O my soul, devoutly think,
   How, with affrighted eyes,
Thou saw'st the wide-extended deep   15
   In all its horrors rise.

Confusion dwelt in every face,
   And fear in every heart ;
When waves on waves, and gulfs on gulfs,
   O'ercame the pilot's art.   20

4 *Omnipotence*, all powerfulness   5 *realms*, kingdoms
11 Switzerland   12 North western coast of Italy
        17 No one knew what to do

Yet then from all my griefs, O Lord,
  Thy mercy set me free ;
Whilst, in the confidence of prayer,
  My soul took hold on Thee.

For though in dreadful whirls we hung   25
  High on the broken wave,
I knew Thou wert not slow to hear,
  Nor impotent to save.

—The storm was laid ; the winds retired,
  Obedient to Thy will ;   30
The sea that roar'd at Thy command,
  At Thy command was still.

                   J. Addison

* 75 *

WRITTEN IN EARLY SPRING.

I HEARD a thousand blended notes
While in a grove I sat reclined,
In that sweet mood when pleasant thoughts
Bring sad thoughts to the mind.

To her fair works did Nature link   5
The human soul that through me ran ;
And much it grieved my heart to think
What Man has made of Man.

Through primrose tufts, in that sweet bower,
The periwinkle trail'd its wreaths ;   10
And 'tis my faith that every flower
Enjoys the air it breathes.

28 *impotent*, unable   29 *laid*, stilled
 1 *blended*, mixed together   2 *reclined*, resting
 3 *mood*, humour   11 *faith*, belief

The birds around me hopp'd and play'd ;
Their thoughts I cannot measure —
But the least motion which they made   15
It seem'd a thrill of pleasure.

The budding twigs spread out their fan
To catch the breezy air ;
And I must think, do all I can,
That there was pleasure there.   20

If this belief from Heaven be sent,
If such be Nature's holy plan,
Have I not reason to lament
What Man has made of Man ?

W. Wordsworth

* 76 *

THE RAINBOW

TRIUMPHAL arch, that fill'st the sky
　　When storms prepare to part,
I ask not proud Philosophy
　　To teach me what thou art.

Still seem, as to my childhood's sight,   5
　　A midway station given,
For happy spirits to alight,
　　Betwixt the earth and heaven.

Can all that optics teach, unfold
　　Thy form to please me so,   10
As when I dreamt of gems and gold
　　Hid in thy radiant bow ?

When science from creation's face
　　Enchantment's veil withdraws,
What lovely visions yield their place   15
　　To cold material laws !

---

1 arch in remembrance of victory   2 *part*, clear off
9 *optics*, laws of sight : *unfold*, explain
14 *enchantment*, the poetry of youth   16 laws of matter

And yet, fair bow, no fabling dreams,
   But words of the Most High,
Have told why first thy robe of beams
   Was woven in the sky.   20

When o'er the green undeluged earth
   Heaven's covenant thou didst shine,
How came the world's gray fathers fo.th
   To watch thy sacred sign !

And when its yellow lustre smiled   25
   O'er mountains yet untrod,
Each mother held aloft her child
   To bless the bow of God.

The earth to thee her incense yields,
   The lark thy welcome sings,   30
When, glittering in the freshen'd fields,
   The snowy mushroom springs.

How glorious is thy girdle, cast
   O'er mountain, tower, and town,
Or mirror'd in the ocean vast   35
   A thousand fathoms down !

As fresh in yon horizon dark,
   As young thy beauties seem,
As when the eagle from the ark
   First sported in thy beam.   40

For, faithful to its sacred page,
   Heaven still·rebuilds thy span ;
Nor lets the type grow pale with age
   That first spoke peace to man.
            T. Campbell

22 *covenant*, sign of peace   23 *gray fathers*, Noah and his family
25 *lustre*, light   29 *incense*, wseetness
32 the mushroom springs up after rain   33 *girdle*, arch, bow
35 *mirror'd*, reflected   42 *span*, arch   43 *type*, sign

* 77 *

TO THE CUCKOO.

HAIL, beauteous stranger of the grove !
  Thou messenger of spring !
Now Heaven repairs thy rural seat,
  And woods thy welcome sing.

What time the daisy decks the green,   5
  Thy certain voice we hear ;
Hast thou a star to guide thy path,
  Or mark the rolling year ?

Delightful visitant, with thee
  I hail the time of flowers,   10
And hear the sound of music sweet
  From birds among the bowers.

The schoolboy wandering through the wood
  To pull the primrose gay,
Starts the new voice of spring to hear,   15
  And imitates thy lay.

What time the pea puts on the bloom
  Thou fliest thy vocal vale,
An annual guest in other lands,
  Another spring to hail.   20

Sweet bird ! thy bower is ever green,
  Thy sky is ever clear ;
Thou hast no sorrow in thy song,
  No winter in thy year !

O could I fly, I'd fly with thee !   25
  We'd make, with joyful wing,
Our annual visit o'er the globe,
  Companions of the spring.

                              J. Logan

3 the trees are in leaf   6 *certain*, sure to come   16 *lay*, song
            18 *vocal vale*, valley where you have sung
                19 a guest who comes every year

* 78 *

TO THE CUCKOO

O BLITHE new-comer ! I have heard,
  I hear thee and rejoice :
O Cuckoo ! shall I call thee bird,
  Or but a wandering Voice ?

While I am lying on the grass   5
  Thy twofold shout I hear ;
From hill to hill it seems to pass,
  At once far off and near.

Though babbling only to the vale
  Of sunshine and of flowers,   10
Thou bringest unto me a tale
  Of visionary hours.

Thrice welcome, darling of the Spring !
  Even yet thou art to me
. No bird, but an invisible thing —   15
  A voice, a mystery ;

The same whom in my schoolboy days
  I listen'd to ; that Cry
Which made me look a thousand ways
  In bush, and tree, and sky.   20

To seek thee did I often rove
  Through woods and on the green ;
And thou wert still a hope, a love ;
  Still long'd for, never seen !

And I can listen to thee yet ;   25
  Can lie upon the plain
And listen, till I do beget
  That golden time again.
    27, 28 *till*, until I fancy myself young again

O blessèd bird ! the earth we pace
Again appears to be   30
An unsubstantial fairy place
That is fit home for Thee !

W. Wordsworth

* 79 *

TO A WATERFOWL

WHITHER, 'midst falling dew,
While glow the heavens with the last steps of day,
Far through their rosy depths, dost thou pursue
Thy solitary way?

Vainly the fowler's eye   5
Might mark thy distant flight to do thee wrong,
As, darkly painted on the crimson sky,
Thy figure floats along.

Seek'st thou the plashy brink
Of weedy lake, or marge of river wide,   10
Or where the rocking billows rise and sink
On the chafed ocean side?

There is a Power whose care
Teaches thy way along that pathless coast,—
The desert and illimitable air,—   15
Lone wandering, but not lost.

All day thy wings have fann'd,
At that far height, the cold, thin atmosphere ;
Yet stoop not, weary, to the welcome land,
Though the dark night is near.   20

And soon that toil shall end ;
Soon shalt thou find a summer home, and rest
And scream among thy fellows ; reeds shall bend
Soon o'er thy shelter'd nest.

3 *pursue*, follow   5 to shoot thee   10 *marge*, edge
15 *illimitable*, without bounds   18 *atmosphere*, air

Thou'rt gone—the abyss of heaven   25
Hath swallow'd up thy form—yet on my heart
Deeply hath sunk the lesson thou hast given,
    And shall not soon depart.

He, who from zone to zone   [30
Guides through the boundless sky thy certain flight,
In the long way that I must tread alone,
    Will lead my steps aright.

W. C. Bryant

* 80 *

SIGNS OF EVENING

THE sun upon the lake is low,
    The wild birds hush their song ;
The hills have evening's deepest glow,
    Yet Leonard tarries long.
Now all whom varied toil and care   5
    From home and love divide,
In the calm sunset may repair
    Each to the loved one's side.

The noble dame on turret high,
    Who waits her gallant knight,   10
Looks to the western beam to spy
    The flash of armour bright.
The village maid, with hand on brow
    The level ray to shade,
Upon the footpath watches now   15
    For Colin's darkening plaid.

Now to their mates the wild swans row,
    By day they swam apart ;
And to the thicket wanders slow
    The hind beside the hart.   20

---

25 *abyss*, depths   29 *zone*, region of the world   31 through life
    9 *turret*, little tower   14 *level*, setting

The woodlark at his partner's side
     Twitters his closing song—
All meet whom day and care divide,—
     But Leonard tarries long !

Sir W. Scott

* 81 *

ARETHUSA

ARETHUSA arose
     From her couch of snows
In the Acroceraunian mountains,—
     From cloud and from crag
     With many a jag,   5
Shepherding her bright fountains.
     She leapt down the rocks
     With her rainbow locks
Streaming among the streams ;—
     Her steps paved with green   10
     The downward ravine
Which slopes to the western gleams :
     And gliding and springing,
     She went, ever singing,
In murmurs as soft as sleep ;   15
     The Earth seem'd to love her,
     And Heaven smiled above her,
As she linger'd towards the deep.

     Then Alphéus bold,
     On his glacier cold,   20
With his trident the mountains strook ;
     And open'd a chasm
     In the rocks ; with the spasm
All Erymanthus shook.

---

3 *Acroceraunian*, see end   6 *shepherding*, leading
          8 little rainbows appear in the spray
11 *ravine*, mountain-valley   21 *trident*, fork with three prongs
          22 *chasm*, rent   23 *spasm*, shock

And the black south wind   25
It conceal'd behind
The urns of the silent snow,
And earthquake and thunder
Did rend in sunder
The bars of the springs below :   30
The beard and the hair
Of the river God were
Seen through the torrent's sweep,
As he follow'd the light
Of the fleet nymph's flight   35
To the brink of the Dorian deep.

'Oh, save me ! Oh, guide me !
'And bid the deep hide me,
'For he grasps me now by the hair !'
The loud Ocean heard,   40
To its blue depth stirr'd,
And divided at her prayer ;
And under the water
The Earth's white daughter
Fled like a sunny beam ;   45
Behind her descended
Her billows, unblended
With the brackish Dorian stream :
Like a gloomy stain
On the emerald main   50
Alphéns rush'd behind,—
As an eagle pursuing
A dove to its ruin
Down the streams of the cloudy wind.

Under the bowers   55
Where the Ocean Powers
Sit on their pearléd thrones :

35 *nymph*, girl-goddess   44 Arethusa   47 *unblended*, not mixed
48 *brackish*, saltish   50 *emerald*, ear green   56 *Powers*, gods

K

Through the coral woods
Of the weltering floods,
Over heaps of unvalued stones ;   60
Through the dim beams
Which amid the streams
Weave a net-work of colour'd light ;
And under the caves,
Where the shadowy waves   65
Are as green as the forest's night :—
Outspeeding the shark
And the sword-fish dark,
Under the ocean foam,
And up through the rifts   70
Of the mountain clifts ;
They pass'd to their Dorian home.

And now from their fountains
In Enna's mountains,
Down one vale where the morning basks,   75
Like friends once parted
Grown single-hearted,
They ply their watery tasks.
At sunrise they leap
From their cradles steep   80
In the cave of the shelving hill ;
At noon-tide they flow
Through the woods below
And the meadows of Asphodel ;
And at night they sleep   85
In the rocking deep
Beneath the Ortygian shore ;—
Like spirits that lie
In the azure sky
When they love but live no more.   90

P. B. Shelley

58 *woods*, coral grows like a tree beneath the water
59 *weltering*, rolling   72 *Dorian*, in Sicily
84 *Asphodel*, probably meadow-narcissus

* 82 *

L'ALLEGRO

HENCE, loathéd Melancholy,
  Of Cerberus and blackest Midnight born
In Stygian cave forlorn
  'Mongst horrid shapes, and shrieks, and sights
    unholy !
Find out some uncouth cell   5
  Where brooding Darkness spreads his jealous
    wings
And the night-raven sings ;
  There under ebon shades, and low-brow'd rocks
As ragged as thy locks,
  In dark Cimmerian desert ever dwell.   10

    But come, thou Goddess fair and free,
    In heaven yclept Euphrosyné,
    And by men, heart-easing Mirth,
    Whom lovely Venus at a birth
    With two sister Graces more   15
    To ivy-crownéd Bacchus bore :
    Or whether (as some sager sing)
    The frolic wind that breathes the spring
    Zephyr, with Aurora playing,
    As he met her once a-Maying—   20
    There on beds of violets blue
    And fresh-blown roses wash'd in dew
    Fill'd her with thee, a daughter fair,
    So buxom, blithe, and debonair.
      Haste thee, Nymph, and bring with thee 25
    Jest, and youthful jollity,
    Quips, and cranks, and wanton wiles,

L'Allegro, the Cheerful man ; pronounce *A laygro*
  2 *Cerberus*, the fabled Dog of the dead   3 *Stygian*, gloomy
  8 *ebon*, black   10 *Cimmerian*, Northern, gloomy
  12 *yclept*, called   24 *debonair*, handsome
  25 *Nymph*, maiden   27 smart and odd turns of speech
                                        K 2

Nods, and becks, and wreathéd smiles
Such as hang on Hebe's cheek,
And love to live in dimple sleek ;   30
Sport that wrinkled Care derides,
And Laughter holding both his sides :—
Come, and trip it as you go
On the light fantastic toe ;
And in thy right hand lead with thee   35
The mountain nymph, sweet Liberty ;
And if I give thee honour due
Mirth, admit me of thy crew,
To live with her, and live with thee
In unreprovéd pleasures free ;   40
To hear the lark begin his flight
And singing startle the dull night
From his watch-tower in the skies,
Till the dappled dawn doth rise ;
Then to come, in spite of sorrow,   45
And at my window bid good-morrow
Through the sweetbriar, or the vine,
Or the twisted eglantine :
While the cock with lively din
Scatters the rear of darkness thin,   50
And to the stack, or the barn-door,
Stoutly struts his dames before :
Oft listening how the hounds and horn
Cheerly rouse the slumbering morn:
From the side of some hoar hill,   55
Through the high wood echoing shrill.
Sometime walking, not unseen,
By hedge-row elms, on hillocks green,
Right against the eastern gate
Where the great Sun begins his state   60

29 *Hebe*, Youth   36 see end   40 *unreprovéd*, innocent
45 *eglantine*, dog-rose   52 *dames*, hens
54 seem to waken the day   60 *state*, progress

Robed in flames and amber light ;
The clouds in thousand liveries dight ;
While the ploughman, near at hand,
Whistles o'er the furrow'd land,
And the milkmaid singeth blithe,   65
And the mower whets his scythe,
And every shepherd tells his tale
Under the hawthorn in the dale.
    Straight mine eye hath caught new pleasures
Whilst the landscape round it measures ;   70
Russet lawns, and fallows gray,
Where the nibbling flocks do stray ;
Mountains, on whose barren breast
The labouring clouds do often rest ;
Meadows trim with daisies pied,   75
Shallow brooks, and rivers wide ;
Towers and battlements it sees
Bosom'd high in tufted trees,
Where perhaps some Beauty lies,
The Cynosure of neighbouring eyes.   80
    Hard by, a cottage chimney smokes
From betwixt two agéd oaks,
Where Corydon and Thyrsis, met,
Are at their savoury dinner set
Of herbs, and other country messes   85
Which the neat-handed Phillis dresses ;
And then in haste her bower she leaves
With Thestylis to bind the sheaves ;
Or, if the earlier season lead,
To the tann'd haycock in the mead.   90
    Sometimes with secure delight
The upland hamlets will invite,

---

62 *dight*, dressed   67 *tells his tale*. counts his flock
71 *lawns*, open grass or moorside   75 *pied*, variegated
80 *Cynosure*, Pole-star, to which every one looks up
83 *Corydon, &c.*, poetical names for country-people
90 *tann'd*, turned brown   91 *secure*, free from care

When the merry bells ring round,
And the jocund rebecks sound
To many a youth and many a maid,   95
Dancing in the chequer'd shade;
And young and old come forth to play
On a sun-shine holy-day,
Till the live-long daylight fail:
Then to the spicy nut-brown ale,   100
With stories told of many a feat,
How faery Mab the junkets eat;
She was pinch'd, and pull'd, she said;
And he, by friar's lantern led;
Tells how the drudging Goblin sweat   105
To earn his cream-bowl duly set,
When in one night, ere glimpse of morn,
His shadowy flail hath thresh'd the corn
That ten day-labourers could not end;
Then lies him down the lubber fiend,   110
And, stretch'd out all the chimney's length,
Basks at the fire his hairy strength;
And crop-full out of doors he flings,
Ere the first cock his matin rings.
    Thus done the tales, to bed they creep, 115
By whispering winds soon lull'd asleep.
    Tower'd cities please us then
And the busy hum of men,
Where throngs of knights and barons bold,
In weeds of peace high triumphs hold,   120
With store of ladies, whose bright eyes
Rain influence, and judge the prize
Of wit or arms, while both contend
To win her grace, whom all commend.
There let Hymen oft appear   125
In saffron robe, with taper clear,

91 *rebecks*, small fiddles   102 *junkets*, milk-dainties
104 *friar's lantern*, Will o' the wisp 105 Goblin, Robin Goodfellow
110 *lubber*, lubberly   120 *weeds*, dress: *triumphs*, splendid en-
tertainments   125 *Hymen*, fabled God of Marriage

And pomp, and feast, and revelry,
With mask, and antique pageantry;
Such sights as youthful poets dream
On summer eves by haunted stream.   130
Then to the well-trod stage anon,
If Jonson's learned sock be on,
Or sweetest Shakspeare, Fancy's child,
Warble his native wood-notes wild.
    And ever against eating cares   135
Lap me in soft Lydian airs
Married to immortal verse,
Such as the meeting soul may pierce
In notes, with many a winding bout
Of linkéd sweetness long drawn out ;   140
With wanton heed and giddy cunning,
The melting voice through mazes running,
Untwisting all the chains that tie
The hidden soul of harmony ;
That Orpheus' self may heave his head   145
From golden slumber, on a bed
Of heap'd Elysian flowers, and hear
Such strains as would have won the ear
Of Pluto, to have quite set free
His half-regain'd Eurydicé.   150
    These delights if thou canst give,
Mirth, with thee I mean to live.

                  J. Milton

∗ 83 ∗

IL PENSEROSO

HENCE, vain deluding Joys,
    The brood of Folly without father bred !
How little you bestead
    Or fill the fixéd mind with all your toys !

128 *mask*, sort of play   132 *sock*, Ben Jonson's comedies
136 *Lydian*, light and festive   139 *bout*, turn or strain
145 *Orpheus*, see end *Il Penseroso*, the Pensive or Thoughtful man
  3 *bestead*, avail   4 *toys*, trifles

Dwell in some idle brain,   5
  And fancies fond with gaudy shapes possess
As thick and numberless
  As the gay motes that people the sunbeams,
Or likest hovering dreams
  The fickle pensioners of Morpheus' train.   10

  But hail, thou goddess sage and holy,
Hail, divinest Melancholy !
Whose saintly visage is too bright
To hit the sense of human sight,
And therefore to our weaker view   15
O'erlaid with black, staid Wisdom's hue ;
Black, but such as in esteem
Prince Memnon's sister might beseem,
Or that starr'd Ethiop queen that strove
To set her beauty's praise above   20
The sea nymphs, and their powers offended :
Yet thou art higher far descended :
Thee bright-hair'd Vesta, long of yore,
To solitary Saturn bore ;
His daughter she ; in Saturn's reign   25
Such mixture was not held a stain :
Oft in glimmering bowers and glades
He met her, and in secret shades
Of woody Ida's inmost grove,
While yet there was no fear of Jove.   30
  Come, pensive nun, devout and pure,
Sober, steadfast, and demure,
All in a robe of darkest grain.
Flowing with majestic train,
And sable stole of cypres lawn   35
Over thy decent shoulders drawn :

6 *fond*, foolish : *possess*, fill   9 *likest*, most like
10 *pensioners*, followers : *Morpheus*, sleep   14 to be visible
16 *staid*, sober   18 an African prince   19 *Queen*, Cassiopeia
31 *nun*, person retired from the world   33 *grain*, dyed stuff
35 *cypres*, crape

Come, but keep thy wonted state,
With even step, and musing gait,
And looks commercing with the skies,
Thy rapt soul sitting in thine eyes :   40
There, held in holy passion still,
Forget thyself to marble, till,
With a sad leaden downward cast,
Thou fix them on the earth as fast :
And join with thee, calm Peace, and Quiet ; 45
Spare Fast, that oft with gods doth diet,
And hears the Muses in a ring
Aye round about Jove's altar sing :
And add to these retired Leisure,
That in trim gardens takes his pleasure :— 50
But first, and chiefest, with thee bring
Him that yon soars on golden wing,
Guiding the fiery-wheeléd throne,
The cherub Contemplatión ;
And the mute Silence hist along,   55
'Less Philomel will deign a song
In her sweetest, saddest plight,
Smoothing the rugged brow of Night,
While Cynthia checks her dragon yoke
Gently o'er the accustom'd oak.   60
—Sweet bird, that shunn'st the noise of folly,
Most musical, most melancholy !
Thee, chauntress, oft, the woods among
I woo, to hear thy even-song ;
And missing thee, I walk unseen   65
On the dry, smooth-shaven green,
To behold the wandering Moon
Riding near her highest noon,

38 *musing gait,* thoughtful pace   39 *commercing,* holding speech
40 *rapt,* tranced   41 *passion,* ecstasy   46 see end
55 *hist,* go quietly   56 *'less,* unless : *Philomel,* nightingale
57 *plight,* state   58 softening the gloom
59 *Cynthia,* Moon ; Milton fancies her in a chariot drawn by two
dragons   63 *chauntress,* singer   64 *woo,* walk and look for

Like one that had been led astray
Through the heaven's wide pathless way   70
And oft, as if her head she bow'd,
Stooping through a fleecy cloud.
   Oft, on a plat of rising ground
I hear the far-off curfeu sound
Over some wide-water'd shore,   75
Swinging slow with sullen roar :
Or, if the air will not permit,
Some still removéd place will fit,
Where glowing embers through the room
Teach light to counterfeit a gloom ;   80
Far from all resort of mirth,
Save the cricket on the hearth,
Or the bellman's drowsy charm
To bless the doors from nightly harm.
   Or let my lamp at midnight hour   85
Be seen in some high lonely tower,
Where I may oft out-watch the Bear
With thrice-great Hermes, or unsphere
The spirit of Plato, to unfold
What worlds or what vast regions hold   90
The immortal mind, that hath forsook
Her mansion in this fleshly nook :
And of those demons that are found
In fire, air, flood, or under ground,
Whose power hath a true consent   95
With planet, or with element.
Sometime let gorgeous Tragedy
In scepter'd pall come sweeping by,
Presenting Thebes, or Pelops' line,
Or the tale of Troy divine ;   100

74 *curfeu*, evening bell   80 serve to show the darkness
87 sit up all night   88-9, *Hermes, Plato,* ancient philo-
sophers: *unsphere*, bring down upon earth   92 *nook*, the body
95 *consent*, agreement   96 with the stars and the forces of Nature
98 see end

Or what (though rare) of later age
Ennobled hath the buskin'd stage.
　　But, O sad Virgin, that thy power
Might raise Musaeus from his bower,
Or bid the soul of Orpheus sing　　　　105
Such notes as, warbled to the string,
Drew iron tears down Pluto's cheek
And made Hell grant what Love did seek
Or call up him that left half-told
The story of Cambuscan bold,　　　　110
Of Camball, and of Algarsife,
And who had Canacé to wife
That own'd the virtuous ring and glass ;
And of the wondrous horse of brass
On which the Tartar king did ride :　　　115
And if aught else great bards beside
In sage and solemn tunes have sung
Of turneys, and of trophies hung,
Of forests, and enchantments drear,
Where more is meant than meets the ear.　120
　　Thus, Night, oft see me in thy pale career,
Till civil-suited Morn appear,
Not trick'd and frounced as she was wont
With the Attic Boy to hunt,
But kercheft in a comely cloud　　　　125
While rocking winds are piping loud,
Or usher'd with a shower still,
When the gust hath blown his fill,
Ending on the rustling leaves
With minute-drops from off the eaves.　　130
And when the sun begins to fling
His flaring beams, me, Goddess, bring

---

104 *Musaeus*, a fabled poet　　109 *him*, Chaucer, in his unfinished
Squire's Tale　　　　118 *turneys*, solemn fights : *trophies*,
armour and weapons of defeated enemies　　121 *career*, course
122 *civil-suited*, peacefully dressed　　123 *frounced*, curled
124 *Boy*, Cephalus, supposed husband to the Dawning
125 *kercheft*, hooded　　　　127 *usher'd*, led in

To archéd walks of twilight groves,
And shadows brown, that Sylvan loves,
Of pine, or monumental oak,   135
Where the rude axe, with heavéd stroke,
Was never heard the nymphs to daunt
Or fright them from their hallow'd haunt.
There in close covert by some brook
Where no profaner eye may look,   140
Hide me from day's garish eye,
While the bee with honey'd thigh
That at her flowery work doth sing,
And the waters murmuring,
With such concert as they keep   145
Entice the dewy-feather'd Sleep ;
And let some strange mysterious dream
Wave at his wings in aery stream
Of lively portraiture display'd,
Softly on my eyelids laid :   150
And, as I wake, sweet music breathe
Above, about, or underneath,
Sent by some spirit to mortals good,
Or the unseen Genius of the wood.
    But let my due feet never fail   155
To walk the studious cloister's pale,
And love the high-embowéd roof,
With antique pillars massy proof,
And storied windows richly dight,
Casting a dim religious light :   160
There let the pealing organ blow
To the full-voiced quire below
In service high and anthems clear,
As may with sweetness, through mine ear,

134 *Sylvan*, fabled God of the woods   137 *nymphs*, wood-fairies
    141 *garish*, staring   154 *Genius*, Spirit
    156 *pale*, enclosure   157 Gothic vaulting
    158 *massy*. massive   159 *dight*, adorned

Dissolve me into ecstasies, 165
And bring all Heaven before mine eyes.
   And may at last my weary age
Find out the peaceful hermitage,
The hairy gown and mossy cell,
Where I may sit and rightly spell 170
Of every star that heaven doth show,
And every herb that sips the dew ;
Till old experience do attain
To something like prophetic strain.
   These pleasures, Melancholy, give, 175
And I with thee will choose to live.

J. Milton

· 84 ·

A HAPPY OLD AGE

HAPPY were he could finish forth his fate
In some unhaunted desert, where, obscure
From all society, from love and hate
Of worldly folk, there should he sleep secure ;

Then wake again, and yield God ever praise ; 5
Content with hip, with haws, and brambleberry ;
In contemplation passing still his days,
And change of holy thoughts to make him merry :

Who, when he dies, his tomb might be the bush
Where harmless robin resteth with the thrush : 10
   —Happy were he !

R. Devereux, Earl of Essex

170 *spell*, study   1 *he could*, he who could end his life
2 *unhaunted*, unpeopled : *obscure*, hidden
8 *merry*, cheer him up

* 85 *

A CRADLE SONG

WHAT does little birdie say
In her nest at peep of day?
Let me fly, says little birdie,
Mother, let me fly away.
Birdie, rest a little longer,
Till the little wings are stronger.
So she rests a little longer,
Then she flies away

What does little baby say,
In her bed at peep of day?
Baby says, like little birdie,
Let me rise and fly away.
Baby, sleep a little longer,
Till the little limbs are stronger.
If she sleeps a little longer,
Baby too shall fly away.

Lord Tennyson

* 86 *

THE DYING SWAN

I

THE plain was grassy, wild and bare,
Wide, wild, and open to the air,
Which had built up everywhere
 An under-roof of doleful gray.
With an inner voice the river ran,
Adown it floated a dying swan,
 And loudly did lament.
 It was the middle of the day.
Ever the weary wind went on,
 And took the reed-tops as it went.

II

Some blue peaks in the distance rose,
And white against the cold-white sky,
Shone out their crowning snows.
   One willow over the river wept,
And shook the wave as the wind did sigh ;   15
Above in the wind was the swallow,
      Chasing itself at its own wild will,
      And far thro' the marish green and still
      The tangled water-courses slept,
Shot over with purple, and green, and yellow.   20

III

The wild swan's death-hymn took the soul
Of that waste place with joy
Hidden in sorrow : at first to the ear
The warble was low, and full and clear ;
And floating about the under-sky,   25
·Prevailing in weakness, the coronach stole
Sometimes afar, and sometimes anear ;
But anon her awful jubilant voice,
With a music strange and manifold,
Flow'd forth on a carol free and bold ;   30
As when a mighty people rejoice
With shawms, and with cymbals, and harps of gold,
And the tumult of their acclaim is roll'd
Thro' the open gates of the city afar,
To the shepherd who watcheth the evening star. 35

18 *marish*, marsh   21 *took the soul*, filled and penetrated
26 *coronach*, Gaelic word for *death-wail*   28 *jubilant*, rejoicing
triumphantly   32 *shawms* and *cymbals*, musical instruments
33 *acclaim*, sound

And the creeping mosses and clambering weeds,
And the willow-branches hoar and dank,
And the wavy swell of the soughing reeds,
And the wave-worn horns of the echoing bank,
And the silvery marish-flowers that throng   40
The desolate creeks and pools among,
Were flooded over with eddying song.

Lord Tennyson

⁙ 87 ⁙

THE BEGGAR MAID

HER arms across her breast she laid ;
   She was more fair than words can say :
Bare-footed came the beggar maid
   Before the king Cophetua.
In robe and crown the king stept down,   5
   To meet and greet her on her way ;
' It is no wonder,' said the lords,
   ' She is more beautiful than day.'

As shines the moon in clouded skies,
   She in her poor attire was seen :   10
One praised her ancles, one her eyes,
   One her dark hair and lovesome mien.
So sweet a face, such angel grace,
   In all that land had never been :
Cophetua sware a royal oath :   15
   ' This beggar maid shall be my queen !'

Lord Tennyson

38 *soughing*, sighing   39 *horns*, little projections or capes
10 *attire*, dress   12 *lovesome mien*, loveable look

· 88 ·

THE LORD OF BURLEIGH

In her ear he whispers gaily,
  'If my heart by signs can tell,
Maiden, I have watch'd thee daily,
  And I think thou lov'st me well.'
She replies, in accents fainter,   5
  'There is none I love like thee.'
He is but a landscape-painter,
  And a village maiden she.
He to lips, that fondly falter,
  Presses his without reproof: 10
Leads her to the village altar,
  And they leave her father's roof.
'I can make no marriage present:
  Little can I give my wife.
Love will make our cottage pleasant,   15
  And I love thee more than life.'
They by parks and lodges going
  See the lordly castles stand:
Summer woods, about them blowing,
  Made a murmur in the land.   20
From deep thought himself he rouses,
  Says to her that loves him well,
'Let us see these handsome houses
  Where the wealthy nobles dwell.'
So she goes by him attended,   25
  Hears him lovingly converse,
Sees whatever fair and splendid
  Lay betwixt his home and hers;
Parks with oak and chestnut shady,
  Parks and order'd gardens great,   30
Ancient homes of lord and lady,
  Built for pleasure and for state.

26 *converse*, talk   32 *state*, grandeur

L

All he shows her makes him dearer :
    Evermore she seems to gaze
On that cottage growing nearer,   35
    Where they twain will spend their days.
O but she will love him truly !
    He shall have a cheerful home ;
She will order all things duly,
    When beneath his roof they come.   40
Thus her heart rejoices greatly,
    Till a gateway she discerns
With armorial bearings stately,
    And beneath the gate she turns ;
Sees a mansion more majestic   45
    Than all those she saw before :
Many a gallant gay domestic
    Bows before him at the door.
And they speak in gentle murmur,
    When they answer to his call,   50
While he treads with footstep firmer,
    Leading on from hall to hall.
And, while now she wonders blindly,
    Nor the meaning can divine,
Proudly turns he round and kindly,   55
    'All of this is mine and thine.'
Here he lives in state and bounty,
    Lord of Burleigh, fair and free,
Not a lord in all the county
    Is so great a lord as he.   60
All at once the colour flushes
    Her sweet face from brow to chin :
As it were with shame she blushes,
    And her spirit changed within.
Then her countenance all over   65
    Pale again as death did prove :

36 *twain*, two   43 *armorial bearings*, carved coat-of-arms
47 *domestic*, (man) servant   54 *divine*, make out

But he clasp'd her like a lover,
　　And he cheer'd her soul with love.
So she strove against her weakness,
　　Tho' at times her spirit sank :　　　　70
Shaped her heart with woman's meekness
　　To all duties of her rank :
And a gentle consort made he,
　　And her gentle mind was such
That she grew a noble lady,　　　　　　75
　　And the people loved her much.
But a trouble weigh'd upon her,
　　And perplex'd her, night and morn,
With the burthen of an honour
　　Unto which she was not born.　　　　8o
Faint she grew, and ever fainter,
　　And she murmur'd, ' Oh, that he
Were once more that landscape-painter,
　　Which did win my heart from me !'
So she droop'd and droop'd before him,　　85
　　Fading slowly from his side :
Three fair children first she bore him,
　　Then before her time she died.
Weeping, weeping late and early,
　　Walking up and pacing down,　　　　90
Deeply mourn'd the Lord of Burleigh,
　　Burleigh-house by Stamford-town.
And he came to look upon her,
　　And he look'd at her and said,
' Bring the dress and put it on her,　　　95
　　That she wore when she was wed.'
Then her people, softly treading,
　　Bore to earth her body, drest
In the dress that she was wed in,
　　That her spirit might have rest.　　　1oo

Lord Tennyson

73 *consort*, wife　　　　78 *perplexed*, puzzled

L .

* 89 *

THE LADY OF SHALOTT

I

ON either side the river lie
Long fields of barley and of rye,
That clothe the wold and meet the sky ;
And thro' the field the road runs by
     To many-tower'd Camelot ;   5
And up and down the people go,
Gazing where the lilies blow
Round an island there below,
     The island of Shalott.

Willows whiten, aspens quiver,   10
Little breezes dusk and shiver
Thro' the wave that runs for ever
By the island in the river
     Flowing down to Camelot.
Four gray walls, and four gray towers,   15
Overlook a space of flowers,
And the silent isle imbowers
     The Lady of Shalott.

By the margin, willow-veil'd,
Slide the heavy barges trail'd   20
By slow horses ; and unhail'd
The shallop flitteth silken-sail'd
     Skimming down to Camelot :
But who hath seen her wave her hand ?
Or at the casement seen her stand ?   25
Or is she known in all the land,
     The Lady of Shalott ?

11 *dusk and shiver*, make the water dusky and bright by turns
17 *imbowers*, forms a bower for   25 *casement*, window

Only reapers, reaping early
In among the bearded barley,
Hear a song that echoes cheerly 30
From the river winding clearly,
    Down to tower'd Camelot:
And by the moon the reaper weary,
Piling sheaves in uplands airy,
Listening, whispers ''Tis the fairy 35
    Lady of Shalott.'

II

THERE she weaves by night and day
A magic web with colours gay.
She has heard a whisper say,
A curse is on her if she stay 40
    To look down to Camelot.
She knows not what the curse may be,
And so she weaveth steadily,
And little other care hath she,
    The Lady of Shalott. 45

And moving thro' a mirror clear
That hangs before her all the year,
Shadows of the world appear.
There she sees the highway near
    Winding down to Camelot: 50
There the river eddy whirls,
And there the surly village-churls,
And the red cloaks of market girls,
    Pass onward from Shalott.

Sometimes a troop of damsels glad, 55
An abbot on an ambling pad,
Sometimes a curly shepherd-lad,
Or long-hair'd page in crimson clad,

---

52 *churls*, country-folk   56 *pad*, path-, or road-horse

Goes by to tower'd Camelot;
And sometimes thro' the mirror blue   60
The knights come riding two and two:
She hath no loyal knight and true,
    The Lady of Shalott.

But in her web she still delights
To weave the mirror's magic sights,   .   65
For often thro' the silent nights
A funeral, with plumes and lights
    And music, went to Camelot:
Or when the moon was overhead,
Came two young lovers lately wed;   70
' I am half sick of shadows,' said
    The Lady of Shalott.

III

A BOW-SHOT from her bower-eaves,
He rode between the barley-sheaves,
The sun came dazzling thro' the leaves,   75
And flamed upon the brazen greaves
    Of bold Sir Lancelot.
A red-cross knight for ever kneel'd
To a lady in his shield,
That sparkled on the yellow field,   80
    Beside remote Shalott.

The gemmy bridle glitter'd free,
Like to some branch of stars we see
Hung in the golden Galaxy.
The bridle bells rang merrily   85
    As he rode down to Camelot:

76 *greaves*, armour for the legs   79 *in his shield*, painted upon it
84 *Galaxy*, the Milky Way among the stars

And from his blazon'd baldric slung
A mighty silver bugle hung,
And as he rode his armour rung,
    Beside remote Shalott. 90

All in the blue unclouded weather
Thick-jewell'd shone the saddle-leather,
The helmet and the helmet-feather
Burn'd like one burning flame together,
    As he rode down to Camelot. 95
As often thro' the purple night,
Below the starry clusters bright,
Some bearded meteor, trailing light,
    Moves over still Shalott.

His broad clear brow in sunlight glow'd ; 100
On burnish'd hooves his war-horse trode ;
From underneath his helmet flow'd
His coal-black curls as on he rode,
    As he rode down to Camelot.
From the bank and from the river 105
He flash'd into the crystal mirror,
'Tirra lirra,' by the river
    Sang Sir Lancelot.

She left the web, she left the loom,
She made three paces thro' the room, 110
She saw the water-lily bloom,
She saw the helmet and the plume,
    She look'd down to Camelot.
Out flew the web and floated wide ;
The mirror crack'd from side to side ; 115
' The curse is come upon me,' cried
    The Lady of Shalott.

87 *baldric*, girdle, belt   98 *bearded*, with a trail of light

IV

IN the stormy east-wind straining,
The pale yellow woods were waning,
The broad stream in his banks complaining,   120
Heavily the low sky raining
    Over tower'd Camelot ;
Down she came and found a boat
Beneath a willow left afloat,
And round about the prow she wrote   125
    The Lady of Shalott.

And down the river's dim expanse
Like some bold seër in a trance,
Seeing all his own mischance—
With a glassy countenance   130
    Did she look to Camelot.
And at the closing of the day
She loosed the chain, and down she lay ;
The broad stream bore her far away,
    The Lady of Shalott.   135

Lying, robed in snowy white
That loosely flew to left and right—
The leaves upon her falling light—
Thro' the noises of the night
    She floated down to Camelot :   140
And as the boat-head wound along
The willowy hills and fields among,
They heard her singing her last song,
    The Lady of Shalott.

Heard a carol, mournful, holy,   145
Chanted loudly, chanted lowly,
Till her blood was frozen slowly,
And her eyes were darken'd wholly,
    Turn'd to tower'd Camelot.

128 *seer*, magician

For ere she reach'd upon the tide 150
The first house by the water-side,
Singing in her song she died,
    The Lady of Shalott.

Under tower and balcony,
By garden-wall and gallery, 155
A gleaming shape she floated by,
Dead-pale between the houses high,
    Silent into Camelot.
Out upon the wharfs they came,
Knight and burgher, lord and dame, 160
And round the prow they read her name,
    The Lady of Shalott.

Who is this? and what is here?
And in the lighted palace near
Died the sound of royal cheer; 165
And they cross'd themselves for fear,
    All the knights at Camelot:
But Lancelot mused a little space;
He said, 'She has a lovely face;
God in his mercy lend her grace, 170
    The Lady of Shalott.'

Lord Tennyson

• 90 •

THE CHARGE OF THE LIGHT BRIGADE

I

HALF a league, half a league,
    Half a league onward,
All in the valley of Death
    Rode the six hundred.
'Forward, the Light Brigade! 5
Charge for the guns!' he said:
Into the valley of Death
    Rode the six hundred.

1 *league*, three miles

II

' Forward, the Light Brigade ! '
Was there a man dismay'd?   10
Not tho' the soldier knew
    Some one had blunder'd :
Their's not to make reply,
Their's not to reason why,
Their's but to do and die :   15
Into the valley of Death
    Rode the six hundred.

III

Cannon to right of them,
Cannon to left of them,
Cannon in front of them   20
    Volley'd and thunder'd ;
Storm'd at with shot and shell,
Boldly they rode and well,
Into the jaws of Death,
Into the mouth of Hell   25
    Rode the six hundred.

IV

Flash'd all their sabres bare,
Flash'd as they turn'd in air
Sabring the gunners there,
Charging an army, while   30
    All the world wonder'd :
Plunged in the battery-smoke
Right thro' the line they broke ;
Cossack and Russian
Reel'd from the sabre-stroke   35
    Shatter'd and sunder'd.
Then they rode back, but not
    Not the six hundred.

35 *sundered*, divided

V

Cannon to right of them,
Cannon to left of them,   40
Cannon behind them
   Volley'd and thunder'd ;
Storm'd at with shot and shell,
While horse and hero fell,
They that had fought so well   45
Came thro' the jaws of Death,
Back from the mouth of Hell,
All that was left of them,
   Left of six hundred.

VI

When can their glory fade?   50
O the wild charge they made !
   All the world wonder'd.
Honour the charge they made !
Honour the Light Brigade,
   Noble six hundred !   55

Lord Tennyson

End of First Part

NOTES:

MAINLY HISTORICAL AND CRITICAL

PAGE	NO.	
6	4	Most copies of Cowper's poems contain an account of these hares, written in the exquisite prose of which he was master.
13	9	The poetry which Blake, an artist of very high and rare powers, wrote during his youth, shows the same qualities as his art : simple yet often majestic imagination, spiritual insight, profound feeling for grace and colour. Like his art also, his verse is narrow in its range, and at times eccentric to the neighbourhood of madness. But, whatever he writes, his eye is always straight upon his subject.
26	12	So many beautiful pieces in prose and verse have been written in the Scots or North Country language that a great source of pleasure is lost by readers who will not take the small pains required to master the peculiarities of spelling and vocabulary : it is hoped that the very numerous notes added here will tempt children to give themselves this pleasure.
		The original ballads by unknown poets appear generally to have taken their present form within the two hundred years before 1700.
33	16	Casabianca was son to a French Admiral commanding the flag-ship *L'Orient* at the battle of the Nile, 1798.
34	17	The *Birkenhead*, steam troop-ship, struck near Simon's Bay, Cape of Good Hope, 25th of February, 1852. Four hundred and thirty-eight officers, soldiers, and seamen, were lost : including the military commander, Colonel Seton of the 74th. For some alterations which make this fine poem more intelligible to children, readers are indebted to the author's kindness.
37	19	These gallant lines are almost worthy of Campbell.
33	20	The *Royal George*, of 108 guns, commanded by Admiral Kempenfelt, whilst undergoing a partial careening in Portsmouth Harbour, was overset about 10 A.M. Aug. 29 1782. The total loss was believed to be near 1,000 souls. These lines were written (Sept. 1782) to the music of the March in Handel's *Scipio*. For tenderness and grandeur under the form of severe simplicity they have few rivals. They are Greek after the manner in which a modern English poet should be Greek :—Readers who admire them are on the right way to high and lasting pleasure.
39	21	Burns justly named this 'one of the most beautiful songs in the Scots or any other language.'
41	23	'I never saw anything like this funeral dirge,' says Charles Lamb, 'except the ditty which reminds Ferdinand of his drowned father in the *Tempest*. As that is of the water, watery ; so this is of the earth, earthy. Both have that intenseness of feeling, which seems to resolve itself into the element which it contemplates.'
42	24	Alexander Selkirk's life of four years in the desolate

PAGE NO.

island, *Juan Fernandez*, may have been in De Foe's mind when he wrote 'Robinson Crusoe.'

48 28 Line 66, *Cockrood*, unexplained, so far as the Editor can learn. It would seem to mean either a *road* or *run*, as we say, for woodcocks ; or a wooden stage for them, by a vague use of *rood*.

49 29 A justly famous specimen of the allegorical style prevalent in Elizabeth's time: the Shepherd's life being poetically glorified and described as a type of life in general. This piece should be compared with the charming truthfulness of Herrick's country scenes in the preceding piece, or Wordsworth's following :—Marlowe's has much beauty : but how much more beautiful is Truth, in the hands of a genuine poet !

68 41 The tale of Lord Leicester's private marriage with Amy Robsart, her imprisonment and fearful death at Cumnor Hall, near Oxford, partially confirmed by history, has been made more real to us than most historical realities by Sir Walter Scott's *Kenilworth :* the most splendid of the three tragic romances left by that great writer.

78 47 This spirited poem, which blazes throughout with the highhearted patriotism of its distinguished author, should be read accompanied by some history of the period, and the map of England.

Line 10, *Pinta;* the Editor can find no Spanish vessel recorded under this name ; nor does the word, in Spanish, bear any sense applicable to a ship. Medina Sidonia, who commanded the Armada, sailed in the *Saint Martin.*

Line 23, At Cressy, in Picardy, the king of Bohemia, and a body of Genoese soldiers, fought in the army of Philip. *Cæsar's eagle shield* appears to be an allusion to some German troops who also served. The eagle is the ancient bearing of the empire.

Line 42, Mines of lead and zinc exist in the Mendip Hills.

Line 43, *Longleat, Cranbourne;* houses in Wilts and Dorset belonging to Lords Bath and Salisbury.

Line 71, *Belvoir*, house of the Duke of Rutland near Grantham.

Line 73, *Gaunt's embattled pile*, Lancaster Castle, built by John of Gaunt about 1363.

82 48 This battle was fought December 2, 1800, between the Austrians under Archduke John and the French under Moreau, in a forest near Munich. *Hohen Linden* means *High Limetrees.*

86 51 Belisarius, a Thracian peasant, became general of the Roman Empire under Justinian. He fought against the Vandals, Moors, Goths, Bulgarians, and other enemies ; but was finally dismissed ungratefully by the Emperor, and died A.D. 565.

The writer of this rough, but truly noble and original poem, died soon after 1800. The version here given (from Plumtre's 'Songs,' 1806) differs from that published by Collins in his very rare little book, 'Scripscrapologia,' 1804.

89 53 Lines 22, 24, These places are in the S.W. promontory of

PAGE	NO.	
		Donegal, Ireland. *Slieveleague* is a mountain ; *Columb-kill* a glen between Slieveleague and the *Rosses* islands.
96	56	The poet professed that these fine, wildly musical lines came to him in his sleep, and that all he did on waking was to write them down. Coleridge, in his magic world, is the most imaginative and romantic of all our poets, Shakespeare (always exceptional) excepted. Seeing how little he wrote in this class, we must regret that he did not dream oftener.
100	59	In this one poem the Editor has ventured to make some changes, in order to simplify the language, which (in the original) does not appear to him to do full justice to the admirable simplicity and pathos of the picture presented.
102	60	During the last three centuries, the poetry written in the North Country or Scots form of English has been so much more important than that written in other forms, as to obscure the peculiar merits which each of them possesses. But the series of poems from which this piece and the next are taken proves the pathos and picturesqueness which the Dorset dialect has when handled by a gifted countryman.
105	62	The death of a young man wandering on Helvellyn in the Lake country, in 1805, supplied Scott with his subject. In this poem the thoughts are much simpler than the language: a rare fault with Scott, or, indeed, with any really great poet.
112	70	An admirable specimen of the Allegorical style which, under the first two Stuart kings, took the place of the pastoral Elizabethan allegory represented by No. 29. Few poets, in C. Lamb's language, are more 'matterful' than Herbert, or express their thoughts with fewer words, introduced only for ornament or metre's sake.
118	72	Remarkable for its close and scientific enumeration of natural phenomena.
119	73	An extract from the long poem said to have been written by poor Smart when confined as a madman. It is full of glorious wildness and intense imagination. Many of its strange phrases (as line 10 here) might probably be traced to, if not explained by, the writings of the 'mystical' theologians.
120	74	It is remarkable how much Addison here anticipates the exquisite suavity and elegance of Cowper's style in similar pieces.
121	75	Wordsworth has left no more consummate specimen of the singular art by which he presents us with a thought which strikes the mind as, at once, perfectly original, and yet, perfectly familiar. The *Cuckoo* (No. 78), on the other hand, paints a fervour of imaginative delight which would be felt only by a highly poetical nature.
128	81	*Arethusa*, with the two poems which follow it, will probably be found difficult at first reading, and may give older children a glimpse into that world of poetry in general to which this book is meant as an introduction.

Shelley has here put into verse, so brilliant that we easily forgive its occasional commonplace and carelessness of phrase, a Greek mythical legend.

> Divine Alpheus, who by secret sluice
> Stole under seas to meet his Arethuse,

—a river rising near Mount Erymanthus in Arcadia

the ancient central province of Southern Greece, is feigned to pursue the stream Arethusa ; they pass through a rent in Mount Erymanthus, cross under the sea to Sicily (opposite to the coast of Greece), and now form one stream in the harbour of Syracuse (Ortygia). *Acroceraunia*, a mountain tract in Northern Greece, must have been named by Shelley inadvertently, or on account of the resonance of the name. This poem is a fine example of Shelley's singular power in *personification* : he paints the rivers as vividly as if they had been real human creatures.

131   82   *L'Allegro* and *Il Penseroso*. It is a striking proof of Milton's astonishing power, that these, the earliest pure descriptive lyrics in our language, should still remain the best in a style which so many great poets have since attempted. The bright and the thoughtful aspects of nature are their subjects ; but each is preceded by a mythological introduction in a mixed Classical and Italian manner. The meaning of the first is that gaiety is the child of nature and of spring ; of the second, that pensiveness is the daughter of solitude and wisdom.

132   —   Line 36, Milton calls Liberty a *mountain-nymph* in allusion to ancient Greece, Switzerland, and other similar countries in which national freedom has been defended by the hardy inhabitants. Wordsworth has a fine sonnet on this subject.

135   —   Line 132, The *sock* was the low shoe worn by actors in the ancient comedies ; the *buskin* (line 102 of the *Penseroso*, No. 83) the high shoe worn in tragedies, to give the figure a more commanding air.

Line 133. *Fancy*: probably used for what we speak of as Imagination. Milton is here alluding to Shakespeare through the mouth of the ' Cheerful Man ;' he hence refers to Shakespeare's lighter qualities.

Line 145, Orpheus in Greek story was a divine musician who redeemed his wife Eurydice from death (Pluto) by song ; but lost her when on the boundary line of life by turning back to look on her before she had passed it. See also *Penseroso*, No. 83, line 105.

137   83   Line 46, *Spare Fast* : Milton elsewhere has expressed his belief that the mind is made clear and fit for high and divine thoughts by fasting.

138   —   Line 87, The *Great Bear*, in English latitudes being always above the horizon, is here used for Night.

Line 98, *Sceptred pall* : Ancient tragedies turned generally on the fortunes of heroic persons, kings, and gods ; hence the actors appeared robed and with sceptres. *Thebes*, &c. are names referring to the great Athenian tragedies.

139   —   Line 110. *Cambuscan*, &c., these names occur in Chaucer's unfinished ' Squire's Tale.'

Line 116, *Great bards* ; referring to such poets as the Italian Ariosto and Tasso, and to our own Spenser..

142   85   This lovely song is taken from the Idyll *Sea Dreams*.

—   86   Founded on the ancient tale that the Swan sang only once, but sang then with magical beauty, to celebrate its own death.

144   87   An old legend, mentioned by Shakespeare in *Romeo and Juliet*, Act II, Scene i.

145   88   Sarah Higgins, a Shropshire lass, was the *village maiden* here described.   She married the Earl of Exeter, owner of Burleigh House near Stamford, a magnificent building of Queen Elizabeth's time, and died in 1797.   The Lady Sophia Cecil, third of the *fair children* (L. 87) was grandmother to the present (third) Duke of Wellington.

148   89   Founded upon an Italian version of the Arthurian romance, which Tennyson has again rendered, under a very different form, in his Idyll *Lancelot and Elaine*. Line 5, *Camelot*, King Arthur's legendary capital.

153   90   This famous Charge occurred during the battle of Balaclava in the Russian war, 25 October, 1854.   The Charge lasted twenty-five minutes, and left more than two-thirds of our soldiers slain or wounded.

INDEX OF WRITERS

THIRD PERIOD

INDEX OF FIRST LINES

RICHARD CLAY AND SONS, LIMITED, LONDON AND BUNGAY.

www.ingramcontent.com/pod-product-compliance
Lightning Source LLC
Chambersburg PA
CBHW031115020726
47495CB00007B/2212